## Between You and Me

I'd always been lucky Jade. At home, Mum and Dad's perfect princess. At school, teacher's pet and joined-at-the-hip bestest friends with Jack.

Then, that fateful September, it all changed . . .

Sybil, looking as if she'd just climbed out of a rock star's bed, arrived at school. And Jack got the blues so bad it almost broke my heart. Then my art project sent me nosing around in unknown territories. I uncovered a past that included dark, moody Finn and endless secrets.

It was like a jigsaw. And now that the puzzle is solved, the final picture may not be perfect. But, between you and me, I wouldn't change a thing.

Julia Clarke was born in Surrey, England, but spent most of her childhood in Germany and Canada. After leaving school at 16, her love of books led to work in a library. After A levels, she gained a Certificate of Education at Goldsmiths College, University of London. A post-graduate course in drama at the Guildford School of Acting was followed by work in all branches of the theatre including writing and performing educational shows in schools. In between acting jobs she travelled to Afghanistan and India, worked for an astrologer and as a cook on a Scottish island. While appearing at Harrogate Theatre, North Yorkshire, she met her husband, Michael, a journalist. They have two teenage children. Julia started writing while living on an isolated farm when her children were small. In 1999 she gained a Distinction in an MA in Creative Writing from the University of Leeds. She enjoys keeping animals, walking, and going to the theatre. *Between You and Me* is her second novel for Oxford University Press.

# Between You and Me

Other books by Julia Clarke

*Summertime Blues*
*You Lose Some, You Win Some*
*Chasing Rainbows*

# Between You and Me

Julia Clarke

OXFORD
UNIVERSITY PRESS

# OXFORD
## UNIVERSITY PRESS

Great Clarendon Street, Oxford OX2 6DP

Oxford University Press is a department of the University of Oxford.
It furthers the University's objective of excellence in research, scholarship,
and education by publishing worldwide in

Oxford New York
Auckland Bangkok Buenos Aires
Cape Town Chennai Dar es Salaam Delhi Hong Kong Istanbul
Karachi Kolkata Kuala Lumpur Madrid Melbourne Mexico City Mumbai
Nairobi São Paulo Shanghai Taipei Tokyo Toronto

Oxford is a registered trade mark of Oxford University Press
in the UK and in certain other countries

British Library Cataloguing in Publication Data available

ISBN 0 19 275382 7

1 3 5 7 9 10 8 6 4 2

Typeset by AFS Image Setters Ltd, Glasgow

Printed in Great Britain by
Cox & Wyman Ltd, Reading, Berkshire

'It is only with the heart that one can see rightly.'

*The Little Prince,* Antoine de Saint-Exupéry

For Mike with all love

## Prelude

I must be the only person in the world who longs for the summer holidays to finish and for school to start. It's terrible—like some sick joke. There again, anyone who had just spent a week at the seaside with my nana might feel the same. Staying in Nana's immaculate bungalow is the nearest thing to medieval torture the twenty-first century can provide. Having your limbs twisted on the rack is similar to Nana's tongue, which makes you feel as if your head is being stretched off your shoulders as you attempt not to answer back.

Answering back, along with just about every other normal activity in the world, including having fun, is on Nana's banned list. The only things she seems to approve of are: housework (every morning we hoover and dust); watching her neighbours (boring); watching early evening TV, especially the news (mega-boring); and taking the sea air (this means sitting shivering on a bench on the prom watching the world go by—mega-mega-blow-your-brains-out-boring).

Nana's bungalow has amazing views of the sea. From

her sitting room you can watch the rain falling vertically, horizontally, and in mini tornadoes. You can also study the pattern of waves thundering in from the North Sea: white horses, white rhinos, and white dinosaurs (all huge, all foaming, all freezing cold). 'Why is it always like winter over here?' I ask Mum despairingly. Even paddling in August gives me hypothermia.

If I was a fanciful person I could almost imagine that Nana, like some wicked witch, has constructed her very own weather zone on the east coast. A place of ferocious icy winds and clammy sea frets that ensure that our holidays are endurance tests and are in no way pleasurable.

On our first day we walk along the beach, the sand blows sharply into my bare legs and the herring gulls circle above screaming like demons. The wind is so fierce it makes your face feel as if it's being peeled. When we get back Nana says with a satisfied smile, 'There! That will have blown all the cobwebs away. I'm sure you feel better for that!'

'Not really,' I dare to mutter.

'You've made that child soft with all those fancy foreign holidays,' Nana shrieks at Mum. Honestly, any minute I think she's going to ring the NSPCC and report Mum for child neglect—all because I don't think walking around in a force 10 gale is bracing.

'Don't answer back,' Mum pleads, after we get Nana settled watching *Countdown* with a mug of tea and a plate of Jaffa Cakes. But as soon as I go into the sitting room Nana starts again.

'You don't wear sensible clothes, that's your problem. That jumper doesn't cover your kidneys. You want to wrap up properly, our Jade. You haven't got a vest on—have you?' Nana accuses me with narrow eyes. Of course I haven't! (A vest? Give me a break!) I hide in my room and stare out at the grey towering sea and the scudding storm clouds that are sweeping like battle lines across the sky.

And I begin working out how many hours it is until we can go home.

Most years it has been OK because Dad and Jack have come with us. Jack has practically lived with us since his mum asked my mum to bring him home from nursery school for her. Every day Jack used to come to our house to play until his mum arrived home from work. Gradually the time she got back grew later and later. Sometimes he'd only go home to go to bed.

'He may as well move in with you. I hope she pays you for all the food he eats,' Nana would say with a sniff when she came to visit us. Then a couple of years ago Dad built Nana a bungalow on a prime plot overlooking the bay. And the only option was for us to visit her (relief!). It must have cost Dad a fortune to build and fit out her bungalow and she's never thanked him. Dad arranged for her little semi to be sold and kind of pretended that the money she got covered the cost of the bungalow—which it obviously didn't.

Sometimes I think that Dad is the only person in the world who really likes Nana, even though she's his mother-in-law. He insists on calling her 'mother' and kisses her cheek when they meet. Yuk! Mum is scared of her, and I think she's poisonous, but Dad, bless him, never has a bad word to say about Nana. She, on the other hand, never has a good word to say about him. 'He's not as common as he used to be,' is her idea of a compliment.

This year it's terrible without Dad. When he's here he makes jokes and sweetens Nana up a bit. Also she's just a teeny weeny bit scared of him and doesn't dare fly at Mum when he's around. Nana always has a go at Mum when she's on her own. Nothing is ever right. And it really gets on my nerves the way Mum scuttles around Nana like a frightened rabbit.

Mum is totally miserable and drippy without Dad and spends hours in the bathroom hiding from Nana, talking to him on her mobile. I'm miserable too, without Jack, although in a way it's a relief not to have Nana's scrutiny and barbed comments. Nana has always thought it strange and awful that my best friend is a boy and has now started to get really suspicious.

'I won't have any hanky-panky in my house, thank you very much,' she said to us last year, banging her finger down on the table as she said 'hanky-panky'. 'I hope we've got one generation at least who can keep their hands to themselves.' As she said this she gave Mum an awful sideways look that made me wince.

Mum gave Jack and me an agonized glance and I had to bite my tongue to stop myself answering back. At least this year we have been spared Nana's view on current morals and the dangers of boys and girls spending too much time 'messing about'. According to Nana, 'messing about' is what we all get up to when we are not 'working'. She's always going on about devils and idle hands. I'm tempted to ask her how she knows so much about it all—but it would only lead to another row for poor old Mum.

But it's really lonely and boring without Jack. We used to go off together on our bikes and get away from Nana; also we could play cards and Monopoly in the evening. This time it is just the three of us in Nana's unbearably stuffy sitting room listening to the radio. (TV is banned after 9 o'clock because there's too much sex and violence.) Dad has doctored her television so she can't pick up Channel Five just in case she ever turns it on by mistake and has a heart attack.

It is on our last evening that Nana really gets to me. She picks holes in everyone all of the time, but I have generally come off lightest. That's only because I am young and therefore have been around for fewer years to be an irritation to her. We get graded on a kind of nuisance-scale: until Grandad passed away Nana referred to him as 'a thorn in my side' or if she was feeling really dramatic 'the cross I must carry'. Mum—with her blue anxious eyes and permanently worried look—is accused of 'never giving me a moment's peace of mind'. Poor old Dad is guilty of 'being too big for his boots'. Up until now I've generally been told I'm 'spoilt to death'. Not a very serious crime.

But on our last evening Nana looks at me with unusual irritability and says: 'Who does she take after? No one in our family is so small and dark.' The word 'ugly' hangs unspoken in the air for a moment and then Nana continues, 'And where does she get that nose? She doesn't take after him.' (There is a sniff and a pursing of lips as she says 'him'—this is how she refers to Dad now Grandad—poor old geezer—has escaped to heaven.) 'Though I suppose there might be all sorts in his background . . . even a touch of the tar brush,' she adds, scowling at Mum as if all this is somehow her fault.

'We went to Florida for our holiday. The weather was brilliant. Jade is very tanned,' Mum says beseechingly.

But Nana's cruel words have planted a seed in my mind. I sit in the spare room and look at myself in the dressing table mirror. I don't look much like either of my parents. Dad is tall with light brown hair and blue eyes. My eyes are dark brown and my hair is getting darker with each passing year. Frowning at my reflection I find myself wishing I hadn't got so tanned and I didn't look so foreign. I know Dad was brought up in different children's homes. So I don't know anything about his parents. I had assumed he was an orphan because he has never talked about his family. I feel a moment of sudden apprehension. Maybe I have other relatives—worse than Nana—out there. Oh-my-goodness! What a prospect!

I try to smile away my fear. Tomorrow we go home. Monday is school and I will see Jack again. But it is as if Nana has placed a drop of poison in my ear. I look down at my skinny brown arms and then study my profile in the mirror. I feel really dissatisfied with my appearance. But, worse than that, I feel as if Nana has torn a little hole in my soul, a small, ragged hurt, that will not be mended by just forgetting all about it.

# 1

I don't see Jack until the first lesson at school. It's really frustrating not to be able to talk to him. Instead we are stuck in a tutorial lesson and Lucy Holden, the biggest moaner in the world, is complaining to The Frog about her timetable. Jack once described Lucy as having camel lips, so I can't look at her now without smiling. To fill in the time Jack and I pass each other notes.

*'We missed you at Bay View. It was dead boring without you. Nana was complaining my nose is too big!!'*

*'You have a beautiful nose! I missed you too. Love is the thief of time.'*

*'That's wicked! Have you just thought of it? Or is it part of a song or a poem?'*

Jack writes back: *'I don't know. It just popped into my head. Either it's mine or I've just stolen it from someone.'*

Jack writes beautiful stuff: stories, poetry, and songs. Miss Langford, the English teacher, is crazy about him. She goes all gooey when he talks to her. He's gorgeous looking, easily the most handsome boy in the school. When he towers over her, all blond and gangly and earnest, reading his work aloud, she twitters like a canary. The rest of us might as well be dead for all the notice she takes of us. Admittedly most of us write really boring yak—especially Lucy Holden. Her account of 'My Dream Home' could send a whole class of hyperactive kids to sleep. Maybe they should market her on tape. You could probably stop riots with her account of bathroom fittings and matching bed linen.

I want to write something nice to Jack. Something to cheer him up. Despite his tan I know that deep inside he's white and strained and washed out. He's just spent two weeks with his father in France and he always comes back from there completely stressed. And it must be bad if it's worse than a week by the sea with Nana! I can't think of anything which matches 'Love is the thief of time', so I do a quick cartoon of a camel and a frog facing each other and am rewarded by a smile.

Just at that moment Mrs Williams crashes into the room like an ocean liner with a strange girl in tow like a captive tug. Big Willie is formidable and we all sit up a bit straighter and Jack and I shuffle our papers away. The Frog leaps to her feet.

'Good morning, Miss Froggit. New girl for your class—Sybil Turner—Professor and Dr Turner's daughter,' Big Willie adds meaningfully.

The Frog turns pink with pleasure. She teaches science so maybe this is good news. 'How lovely! Welcome, Sybil!' Her smile fades a bit when Big Willie moves her vast bulk, exits in a swish of crimplene, and we get a good view of the girl.

A ripple of amusement and appreciation runs through the class like a shiver. This new girl is sensational looking—long, silver blonde hair, a slim greyhound body. She is wearing a tiny, rather creased, school skirt that would fit a first year. Her long brown legs are as hairless and smooth as a conker.

'Class dismissed,' Miss Froggit croaks. Everyone begins filing past the girl, moving slowly and staring. The Frog says to me: 'Jade, will you please look after Sybil until she knows her way around.' Then she adds tentatively to Sybil's retreating back, 'Sybil! There is just one thing. School rules are that girls must either wear socks or tights and have their hair tied back in class.'

Sybil turns, as if she is on the catwalk, hips jutting

defiantly. 'Socks!' she echoes, as if she's never heard the word before.

'I've got a spare pair in my PE kit,' I say quickly.

'And your hair, Sybil?' The Frog adds rather anxiously. Sybil stands staring straight ahead as if she is deaf and without speech. I rummage in my pencil case and silently hand her a scrunchy. With an audible sigh Sybil pulls her gorgeous hair into an untidy topknot. It looks amazing— as if she's just got out of a rock-star's bed or something. Then she defiantly pulls down the sleeves of her jumper and sticks her thumbs through two holes in the cuffs. She looks as if she's wearing mittens. It's really scruffy. For a moment I feel a pang of pity. My mum wouldn't let me out of the house in a holey jumper and skirt so short it hardly covers your bum.

'Jade will sort you out,' The Frog says in a relieved kind of voice. Sybil gives me a deadeye look as if I am invisible. Sometimes it's hard being teacher's pet.

I trail out of the classroom sandwiched between two tall, beautiful, fair people—Jack and Sybil. I feel like a little dark troll and Nana's unkind words come back to haunt me. Sybil looks straight over my head, as if I am a child, and smiles at Jack. 'Hi,' she says huskily.

'Hi, I'm Jack,' he says smiling.

'Everyone seems very friendly here,' she says graciously.

'Yeah, they're a good crowd. Where did you go to school before?' he asks.

'Rushworth Court—Ladies College. I got expelled.' She gives Jack a sly sideways look as she adds: 'I'm a problem child . . .'

'Aren't we all?' he says with a grin at me.

We don't see Sybil for the rest of the day and I am relieved that my babysitting duties seem to be over. But at the end of school she seeks me out.

'Hi,' I say, a bit reluctantly. 'Did you have a good day? Is there anything I can help you with?'

'No.' Her eyes drift past me, as if she is seeking someone in the crowd. 'See you around,' she adds.

Jack is waiting for me in our usual place. It starts to rain and I pull my umbrella out and hurry over to meet him.

We huddle under my brolly, linking arms, walking quickly. My mum always waits for us down one of the side streets near to the school. We haven't gone very far when I hear my name being called.

Glancing around I see Sybil coming after us. The rain, which has soaked her hair to the colour of old gold, runs in little rivulets down her bare legs.

'Everyone's your friend when you have an umbrella,' Jack mutters.

'Where are you two off to?' she asks.

'Home.' I feel I have to extend the umbrella to her, although there is hardly room for three. As Jack is tallest he moves to the middle and we cling to his arms. The rain is even heavier now, coming down in cold grey sheets. It drips down the back of my collar.

'I'll walk with you, if that's OK,' Sybil says unnecessarily. Then I hear my name being called again. It's Mum—she has a huge golf umbrella and is sprinting towards us as if we are drowning in the Atlantic and she's a lifesaver. Sybil giggles.

'Oh, sweetheart, you're getting wet,' Mum says, holding the umbrella out to me, her face creased with concern. Jack moves forward and takes Mum's arm. We swap umbrellas and set off for the car.

'Does your mother always dress like that?' Sybil asks me with another giggle. Mum is wearing a vivid pink tracksuit with yellow appliqué flowers across the front. Her bright blue trainers match her headband.

'She's been at work,' I say, a bit defensively.

'Where—the big top?' Sybil laughs. I know if I was cool I would laugh too, but I can't.

'She works in a nursery. She says little children like

bright colours and cheerful clothes. She does painting and stuff with them.'

When we reach the car Mum says, 'Would your friend like a lift somewhere?'

'It's OK, I'm not in any rush. No one will be home for hours,' Sybil says. She opens her eyes very wide and smiles at Mum.

'Here, take my umbrella,' I say quickly. But Sybil has touched a nerve in my mother's heart.

'Come back and have some tea with us then,' Mum says kindly, giving me a prompting look.

I open the car door and say, 'Yeah, come on. Mum—this is Sybil—she's new.'

'Yes. I thought so.' Mum is happy as a broody hen now she has us all safe and dry in the shelter of the car. 'I know most of Jadey's friends.'

'Jadey got the job of looking after me. Mrs Williams chose her specially.' Sybil leans so far forward her face is almost on Mum's shoulder and I cringe at her use of my pet name.

'How lovely.' Mum sounds thrilled. 'Jade was made form prefect last year and it was a unanimous vote. We were so pleased for her. It's so nice to be popular, isn't it?'

'Yes, it certainly is,' Sybil says, shooting a wondering glance at me, as if I have grown an extra ear or something freaky.

Sybil goes overboard as soon as we drive through the electric gates at home. Our house *is* lovely. Dad bought the plot, which was once the back garden of a big old house, and designed it. The house stands on the top of one of the high hills overlooking the city. We have a veranda along the front, shutters and a Virginia creeper. Inside is a huge hall with a parquet floor and a curved staircase that sweeps up to the landing. It looks a bit like the set for *Gone with the Wind*. Mum loves living up here. She says at night the lights of the city and the outlines of the mill chimneys look like Switzerland. Dad calls it his eyrie and named it Monteagle House. Everyone who visits says how nice it is. But Sybil goes on so much I begin to get the feeling she might be taking the mickey.

Mum is all pink and pleased by her praise. 'Well, thank you, Sybil. Jade's dad designed and built it so it's just as we want it. Come along to the kitchen and get warm.'

Mum makes us tea, hot chocolate, and cinnamon toast. She always has something especially good for tea on school days and fusses around like we've had a day down a coalmine.

'This is like going to a café!' Sybil says gleefully. 'Do you come for tea every day?' she asks Jack. 'You're on to a cushy number, aren't you?' We all laugh as if this is a joke, although it's not really funny. 'What time do you go home?' she adds, and I quickly change the subject because I know Jack hates to talk about how his mother is always working late. I don't really see that any of it is Sybil's business.

Normally Jack and I crash out in my room and watch TV for a while. But I don't want to take Sybil up there. We hang around for so long in the kitchen Mum starts chopping onions and washing potatoes. 'I'll light the fire in the dining room for you, if you like,' Mum says. 'It's not really cold enough but it makes the whole place feel cosy. I love an open fire, don't you?' she says to Sybil.

For some reason Sybil takes this as an invitation to come into the dining room and spread her books over the table. I am really fed up. I wish she'd go home. I want to talk to Jack on my own.

Dad arrives home. Sybil gets so excited you'd think the Blackpool illuminations had just been switched on. 'You're Jadey's daddy. I've heard such a lot about you!' she wriggles across to shake his hand like an enthusiastic puppy.

'Gawd! What've you been hearing about me?' Dad asks grinning. He kisses me and adds: 'I hope my little princess hasn't been saying I keep her short on dosh and won't let her out late.' He hugs me, but I pull away, embarrassed. I don't really want Sybil to hear me being called princess.

'Oh no, I heard you built this beautiful house. You are *so* clever.'

'Well, it's my trade,' Dad says with a laugh. 'Nothing clever about building a house. That's what I do. I'm just a cockney lad who started out as a chippy and made good. Married the right woman and moved up to Yorkshire, that's when I got lucky.' He kisses my mother. 'Something smells good. What are we having? I could eat the horse and his cart I'm that hungry.'

'Steak and chips. Would you like to stay, dear, there's plenty?' Mum says to Sybil. I hold my breath—willing Sybil to say no.

'Oh no, I don't think I should . . . ' Sybil stares at her hemline and puts her thumbs through the holes in her jumper as if she is cold.

'Stay and have a bit of grub,' Dad says. 'You look as if you could do with feeding up.'

'Well, if you're sure,' Sybil says sweetly, lowering her eyelashes like Bambi.

'How was your day, darlin'?' Dad asks me, when we sit down to eat. Normally I tell Mum and Dad every detail of my day—right down to what I had for lunch. But I don't feel like talking in front of Sybil.

'Just lessons. It's funny being in the sixth form. No science.'

Jack looks at my miserable face and makes an effort to fill the gap in the conversation. He tells us about his holiday, which is good of him because he hates talking about France. Sybil doesn't talk—she just eats. It's amazing the amount she can put away.

'It's nice to see a nipper enjoying her food,' Dad says approvingly. He hates waste of any kind. He looks across at my plate with a frown. We are having chocolate cheesecake and I have flattened mine to try to make it look less.

'It seems a shame to leave that last bit—it doesn't keep, does it?' Sybil says, looking anxiously at the remaining slice on the plate. She has already eaten two pieces. Even Dad seems overawed by her gluttony.

'You must have hollow legs, gal,' he says with a grin, as he passes the dish to her.

We're having coffee when Dad's mobile phone begins to ring. 'Hell!' he says.

'Oh dear,' Mum cries anxiously. Just recently the phone has ruled Dad's life. He spent most of our Florida holiday pacing around the pool, talking into his phone and sweating. Now he goes out into the hall and we hear his voice, tense and curt, giving instructions.

He comes back into the kitchen, looking glum. 'I'm sorry, Princess, I really wanted to hear how school went, your first day in the sixth form and everything, but I've got to go out.'

'Oh, Rick, no,' Mum says. 'Surely it can wait until the morning?'

Dad sighs. 'It's a shark infested ocean out there at the moment and my business is a fat little fish. If I don't get these houses in Halifax finished on time I'm for the high jump. I'll give you two kids a lift home,' he says to Jack and Sybil. 'Save Jade's mum going out again. It's a filthy night.'

Mum seems really depressed. She starts cleaning the kitchen as if it's infested with cockroaches. I escape upstairs and watch TV.

Later Mum comes into my room. 'I've found a spare jumper that's miles too big for you. Do you think you could give it to Sybil tactfully?'

'Mum, for heaven's sake!' I say crossly. 'Her parents are doctors—she doesn't need us giving her clothes.'

'Well, I don't know, poor girl. I can't believe they sent her to school looking like that. Her skirt was barely decent.'

'She likes it like that. She thinks she's sexy,' I say bitterly.

'Oh dear . . . ' Mum says anxiously. 'Well, just take the jumper into school . . .'

'No!' I shout. Then I lock myself in my bathroom and spend ages washing my hair. I have never thought of myself as a jealous person. I have happily shared my life, my possessions, and my parents with Jack for as long as I can remember. But seeing Sybil with Mum and Dad has thrown me into a frenzy of some dark unpleasant emotion.

My spirits are so low I even find myself wondering if Nana would like Sybil. Not in her school skirt, that's for sure! But if Sybil were covered up Nana would probably say, 'You can always see breeding. It's in the bones. Comes from good stock that one.' Nana is always going on about good and bad blood and marrying well. She also thinks that having 'a profession' is wonderful. Mum gets her ears burned off hearing about her cousin Daphne who married 'a professional man'. Nana would be dead impressed by Sybil's family. Sick? Or what? And why should I care?

Angry tears fill my eyes. I try to pretend to myself that it's the shampoo. But the truth is that I really dislike Sybil and I don't know why. Apart from scrapping with the boys at junior school if they were horrible to Jack I have never had any fallings-out. I have always been popular and well liked. In turn I have always treated everyone with amused tolerance, secure in my own safe little world.

But the dark little snag in my soul started by Nana's words—'Who does she take after? And where does she get that nose?'—seems to unravel a little more, as if the fabric that is the essential part of me is being pulled apart. I don't feel confident any more. I feel scared and alone. I creep downstairs hoping Mum will still be up and that she will make me hot chocolate and talk for a bit. But the house is deserted—the only sound is the gusting of the September wind and the machine-gun rattle of rain against the windows. The bad weather seems to have followed us from the east coast like a curse.

I wonder how Dad is getting on and when he will be home. I don't like to think of him walking around a building site on a dark and stormy night, trying to sort out problems. Loneliness washes over me like a long slow wave creeping up over a shoreline. It is too late to ring Jack on his mobile. I curl up in bed and close my eyes, waiting for morning.

# 2

When I was a little girl Nana was always saying: 'Now don't get too excited. Or it will end in tears.' This would be repeated endlessly as we queued for the cinema, or were about to go for a boat ride. I've always thought it was part of Nana's attempt to dumb down life so we didn't have too much fun. But regretfully I have to admit that I have got too excited about going back to school and seeing Jack. It doesn't work out like I thought it would and most of the time I *do* feel like crying.

Jack is depressed, more depressed than I have ever known him. He usually writes a couple of sad songs and then feels better. He always tells me what the problem is and we talk it over. But this time it's different. We don't talk about why he is so sad—he just is—and nothing I do seems to make a difference.

I don't understand it because he says France was OK. From what he tells me he didn't have the usual terrible rows with his father. In fact he seems to have had quite a good time. He's getting on better with his stepmother and her kids and even made some friends while he was there. He's writing to a boy called Xavier who might come to visit. It all sounds fun. Compared to staying with Nana at Bay View it sounds like a rave.

I suppose there might be some new problem with his mother, something he doesn't feel he can talk about. But thinking that makes me feel hurt because Jack and I have never had secrets from each other. Jack is one of those people whose emotions show on his face, so he can't hide the fact that he's unhappy.

I'm not exactly over the moon with life at the moment either. School is weird. The whole place becomes a kind of shrine to Sybil. The boys go crazy for her and Sybil-mania rules. Even the upper sixth boys, who normally treat lower sixth girls as if they are lepers, queue up to ask her out. Not even the girls are immune to her appeal. A whole army of them pull their skirts up, tie their hair in raggedy topknots, and make holes in the cuffs of their jumpers. I could probably auction off the spare PE socks I lent her if she hadn't 'lost' them.

Sybil has all the attraction of arriving on the scene fully formed. Like in the famous picture of Venus arising from the waves, where Venus is born completely female, clothed in a wondrous wrap of hair with a knowledgeable simper on her face. It's like this with Sybil—no one ever saw her when she was a gangly twelve year old with a brace and blackheads.

I am one of the few who isn't a Sybil devotee—she gets on my nerves. I have the feeling all the time that she is laughing at me. When I try to explain to Jack he says, 'But you've always taken the mick out of everyone. Everything is a joke to you.'

I'm famous for my impressions of people and making everyone laugh, so all I can say is, 'It's different when someone does it to your face. If she calls me Jadey one more time I shall explode.'

'She's just desperate for attention,' Jack says. 'If you pretend it doesn't bother you she'll stop doing it.'

I change the subject. I refuse to be like the rest of the school who talk of nothing but Sybil. I persuade Jack to get out his portfolio and show me his project work. I only took art to keep him company and I'm struggling. I'm hoping for inspiration. His work is wicked. Our topic is the living world and he is studying animals. This week he has been down to the animal shelter to sketch the dogs.

'I haven't even thought of a topic yet!' I say despairingly. 'Think of something for me, Jack.'

Jack's done masses of sketches. They are all really good. 'The dogs are only kept for a week,' Jack says sadly.

Most of the dogs have pathetic faces and huge sad eyes. Some look angry and a few look a bit mad—you can see why they have been abandoned. Mostly they just look terrified—as if they know what is in store for them. Apart from one, whose huge face fills a page, who seems to be grinning out at us.

'Is this the one who is too stupid to know he only has seven days left?' I ask, trying to swallow the lump in my throat.

'Yes,' Jack says with a smile. 'He's a real character— part Irish wolfhound, part Irish setter. It was love at first sight. He just stood and watched me while I sketched. Then he barked and whined when I left. It was awful. I would have given anything to bring him out with me. But can you see my mother letting me keep a dog? We'd both end up in a homeless shelter.'

When Jack was younger his mother used to threaten to send him into care because she couldn't cope with working and looking after him. I don't think he's ever forgotten it.

'You and puppy could always come and live with us,' I tease. 'My mum would love it.'

'It's a shame your parents didn't have more kids,' Jack says. Then he adds, 'Why don't you do your childhood as your project? Your folks would like that. You could get out all their old photos and visit the places where you used to live.'

'Yes! I could do a surreal Salvador Dali type portrait of Nana with hedgehogs for hair,' I say gleefully and Jack laughs.

Jack gets out his notebook and writes down a list of ideas for me, while I lean against him. It's like it used to be between us and for the first time in ages I actually feel happy. We walk out of school together, arm in arm, discussing my artwork.

We are brought up short by the sight of Sybil standing at the corner of the road where Mum usually parks. Sybil is waiting for us, that's obvious.

'Hi!' she says, staring at Jack. 'How are you? I never seem to see you around school.'

'We're fine,' I say breezily. Jack is silent.

'My parents are out Friday night,' Sybil says airily. 'I'm having a few people around to chill out. Would you like to come?'

I'm not really sure whether she is asking us both or just Jack. But Jack turns to me and says: 'That should be OK, shouldn't it, Jade? OK. We'll be there,' he says to Sybil. She gives Jack her address—already written out on a piece of paper—and then walks off. She knew he'd say yes!

As soon as she is out of earshot I turn on Jack furiously: 'Why on earth did you agree to that? I don't want to go to Sybil's house.'

Jack just shrugs his shoulders. 'If I don't do it she'll think I'm scared of her.'

'Scared of her!' I echo furiously. 'What absolute rubbish! Why should you be scared of Sybil?'

'I don't know. Just leave it, Jade. It won't hurt to go to her house. I'm just curious—that's all.' Jack is really irritable. And I am too cross to be conciliatory.

'Just remember—curiosity killed the cat,' I snap. And we walk on in frosty silence. It seems Sybil manages to ruin things without even trying.

Dad comes to pick us up because Mum is at the hairdresser's. He drops Jack off at the supermarket where he has a part-time job. 'What's happened to your friend Sybil?' Dad asks me as we pull away. 'Is she going to come to our house again for supper? She could eat for England that one. Bet they never throw anything away in their house.'

'Well, we don't throw much away. You eat it all,' I say to Dad. 'All that bubble and squeak and left over puddings for breakfast. I'll tell you what,' I add, 'if we had a dog we'd never throw anything away. Dogs eat all the scraps—don't they?'

'Yeah, so do pigs but we ain't keeping one of them,' he laughs.

'Could we get a dog?' I ask. Dad looks a bit surprised.

'Yes, of course we could, Princess. I love 'em. But you were always nervous of them when you were a nipper. That's why we never had one. What kind of dog would you like? A nice little poodle? Or a Westie? You know—a little Scottie dog. They make smashing pets for little girls. You don't want anything too big.' Dad is getting enthusiastic. 'Course I'd like a German shepherd or a Dobermann myself. Good guard dogs. But it's your pet, Princess, you must choose. We'll get it for your Christmas present. How about that?'

'Actually I think I'd like to go to the animal rescue place and get an abandoned one,' I say quietly.

Dad frowns. 'You can get all kinds of problems with dogs like that. A bad start is difficult to put right. You want a good pedigree—look at the mother—see the litter and pick the brightest and the best.' He sounds like an echo of Nana.

Like Hitler, Nana thinks only the perfect should procreate. 'People like *that* shouldn't be allowed to have children,' is one of her sayings.

'I don't want a perfectly bred dog,' I say a bit sulkily. 'I want a mongrel. I want one that no one else wants.'

'Generally no one else wants it for a good reason,' Dad says gently. Then he adds, 'We'll talk to your mum about it, Princess. She's the boss—you know that.' He brightens up a bit. 'What would you like to do now? We could go into town and get ourselves some tea. How would a cream cake suit you?'

'I've got homework to do,' I say unsmilingly, still a

bit put out at not getting my own way. 'I've got to sketch all the houses I've lived in. I'm doing a pictorial record of my life. Did we live somewhere before Bridge Road?' The Beck Bridge estate where we used to live is a modern housing estate near to school. Jack still lives there.

Dad looks uncomfortable. 'Yes . . . but I don't think it would make much of a picture.'

'Why not?'

'Your nana used to say I'd dragged your mum down to live in the slums.'

'Oh for heaven's sake!' I say, shocked. 'Where was it?'

'The St Aidan's estate,' he says quietly. 'We shared a flat above a greengrocer. I don't think you'll want to see it, Princess.'

He looks grim. And a flicker of anxiety runs through me, but I ignore it. The St Aidan's estate is the worst in the city. When the documentary makers from London want somewhere really grotty to film they always go there.

'I do want to see it. I really do,' I say. 'It's important for my work. Can we go and have a little look? I just need to do a quick sketch. The light is good today.'

'If that's what you really want, Princess,' he says quietly.

We take the ring road out to the east of the city, past empty mills and factories and rows of old terraced houses that cling to the hillside like blackened wonky teeth.

'This will be a trip down memory lane,' he says after a while, and then adds more cheerfully, 'The old estate may not be very pretty but we had some good times. We lived there until you were nearly two. I worked night and day to move us out to somewhere with a garden. We wanted you to have a sandpit and a swing for your second birthday—and you got 'em,' he adds proudly.

He's right about the estate not being very pretty. It's awful. A rabbit warren of featureless roads filled with row upon row of red brick houses. Some of the houses have rubbish in the gardens and windows boarded up. It's horrible.

Because it is such a warm sunny afternoon there are loads of kids and dogs swarming out of scruffy gardens and on to the road. Dad drives really slowly and the kids stare up at the Range Rover as if we are arriving in a space ship.

In the centre of the estate is a row of old stone terraced shops left over from some bygone age. Some of the shops have been turned into houses, but there is still a bakery, a newsagent, and a Co-op late shop. The shop on the corner is a florist called *Flower Power*.

'Blimey! The old place has been smartened up. Used to be Casey's fruit and veg shop. *Flower Power*. I say! We had the room right at the top. There it is, pet, your first home.' He smiles at me affectionately.

There's a big scruffy car park in front of the shops, where buildings have been pulled down and the site left derelict. Dad nudges the car in slowly, carefully avoiding a gang of lads playing football, and a pack of stray dogs that are running wild among the dustbins. I unwind the window, reluctant to leave the safety of the car and start sketching. The kids are yelling at each other and the air is thick with obscenities. The lads seem to think that if they don't use Anglo-Saxon at least six times in every sentence they might be responsible for the old language dying out completely.

Dad smiles indulgently and says, 'Right load of little street Arabs, aren't they?'

'With a very limited use of vocabulary,' I mutter, arranging my pencils along the dashboard.

'Not their fault, don't know no better,' Dad says.

Next thing I know he is out of the car and talking with the kids. I hope he isn't telling them to go away and shut up because his daughter is a genius and needs peace and quiet to concentrate on a masterpiece. (Although I bet

Michelangelo didn't have people effing and blinding in his ear when he was painting the Sistine Chapel!)

Inspiration is in short supply. I sit and stare at the blank page of my sketchbook, pencil hovering, hearing Dad's deep voice mingling with the shrill tones of the boys. I wonder what he is saying to them because they are laughing. We are parked in the sunshine and without the air conditioning the Range Rover is stuffy. I feel sticky and uncomfortable. I pull off my school jumper and untuck my shirt. I draw a couple of tentative lines and then rub them out.

The shouting has started up again. 'Pass it. Don't hog the ball! You fecking fecker!' someone yells. Looking up I see Dad running with the boys and then someone lobs the ball to him. As I watch Dad bounces the ball up on his knee and then heads it skilfully. It sails in a graceful arc past goalposts made from piled up tracky tops. I close my eyes in exasperation. When I open them again I see him doing a kind of Irish jig in celebration to a roar of approval from the boys. 'Fecking great!' someone shouts, so close they could be in the car with me.

Trying not to scowl I get out of the car and beckon to Dad. He comes jogging over, grinning widely. He's taken off his jacket and rolled up his sleeves, his face is glowing.

'What on earth you think you are doing? You can't just start talking to strange kids and running around playing football with them. You'll get accused of being a paedophile!'

He looks so crestfallen that I feel a sharp moment of pity. 'Can't you just sit in the car and listen to the radio?' I add a little more kindly.

Just at that moment there is a horrible crack like a rifle shot. The noise makes me jump. We spin around to see the kids scattering like mice before a cat. The football is rolling out of the florist's shop doorway. Even from here I can see a thin stream of water following it.

'I've told you kids before not to kick that bloody football anywhere near my shop,' a furious voice yells.

'Oh gawd,' Dad groans.

'It's nothing to do with you,' I say quickly.

'I was showing them how to do headers. Don't have so much control when the ball's in the air. I'll go and explain.'

'I shouldn't bother, let's go home.' The autumn afternoon has clouded over—there is a sudden darkness in the sky as if it might thunder. There seems to be no air to breathe down here in the bottom of the valley. I want to drive home as quickly as possible and get away from this place. I wish I hadn't insisted we come. I can't draw anything at all. I feel oppressed, suffocated, as if claustrophobia has me gripped by the throat.

A woman has emerged from the shop and grabbed the football. She is looking around furiously. I can read the signs. She is desperate for a culprit and someone to vent her rage on. 'Let's go,' I say again, more urgently.

'All my fault. I'll pay for any damage,' Dad calls loudly, making his way across to the woman. He picks his jacket up from the now empty goalpost pile and reaches for his wallet.

The woman is looking at him with a totally startled expression. Obviously thinking he is some kind of nutter. Then her face splits into a huge grin and she lets out this great yell. 'I might have known it would be you causing havoc. Where have you been hiding yourself? It's been trouble free around here since you left.' And then she drops the football, rushes over to Dad and throws her arms around him.

Dad hugs her back and I hear him say excitedly, 'Come and meet our little Jade. You won't recognize her. And what are you doing here anyway? Last thing we heard you were off to the States.'

'It didn't work out. Then Dad died and I came back to help Mam with the business. We thought we would sell up but then I started with the flowers and I haven't looked back.'

'We'd have come and seen you if we'd known you were here.' Dad has taken hold of her arm and is leading her over to me. I am standing with my mouth hanging open. Dad and Mum don't have too many close friends—not ones that Dad hugs, anyway. I've never seen him like this before.

'Princess, this is Nola. She let us share her flat when you were a baby. You were brought up with her little boy. And how is Finn, Nola? Don't know about little boy—he must be nineteen now! It doesn't seem possible,' Dad says wonderingly.

Nola smiles at me. She is very thin, with a bony suntanned face and long, red, curly hair. There is something about her looks and the clothes she is wearing—cropped cotton trousers and an embroidered T-shirt—that seems exotic and foreign. Her accent, when she says hello to me, is very Yorkshire, but there is a soft undercurrent that hints at a different origin.

'Pleased to meet you,' I mutter, as we shake hands.

'Come on in and I'll make us a cup of tea,' Nola says. 'Thirsty work, wrecking the world with a football,' she adds teasingly to Dad.

'I'll pay for any damage, you know that,' Dad says, grinning at her.

'It was only a bucket of carnations got knocked over. Didn't touch the window. I have extra-reinforced glass anyway—you have to around here. They'd nick fresh air this lot!'

Dad and Nola walk over to the shop, laughing together, while I trail behind them. I wish I hadn't suggested this visit. I feel alienated by this place and the feeling that it is part of my past. I wish, foolishly, that my life had started in the neat little house in Bridge Road, where Jack was my neighbour and we had a kitten called Buttons. That was the kind of house you find in a kid's first reader. An ordinary safe house where very ordinary safe people live. I realize that I am scared by this place. Frightened by the atmosphere of anger and poverty which hangs in the air like an invisible fog. I imagine what life would have been like if we had carried on living here. And I don't like what I see—not one little bit.

Nola flips the open sign on the shop to closed, locks the door, and leads us through a dark workroom that smells of flowers. She takes us up a flight of carpetless stairs to a scruffy kind of kitchen where a settee and TV are squashed into one half of the room.

'This old place hasn't changed at all,' Dad says in a delighted voice, as if this is in some way a compliment.

Nola laughs, then she gives me a long searching look. I feel uncomfortable, as if somehow she can read all the uncharitable thoughts inside my head. I am thinking how tatty and horrible everything is here.

'I hope our Finn gets home in time to see you. You've grown into such a beauty. He'd be thrilled to see you. He loved you to bits when you were a babby. Do you know he cried for weeks after you left and prayed every night to Our Lady to bring you back! It was heartbreaking.'

Moving to the window I pretend to look out. But in truth I am anxious to get away from her piercing rather analytical gaze. I feel almost faint with some kind of unknown anxiety. I have stumbled, unwittingly, on a past I had no idea existed, and now I find there is some strange boy who loved me to bits when I was a baby. It all seems odd and incredible. I think about the lads who were playing football, their grating voices, the foul language, and a wave of fastidiousness overwhelms me. I hope we leave before this Finn arrives home. Adoration, at any time in my life, from the kind of boy who lives here, holds no attraction at all.

# 3

The roar of an engine from the backyard of the house makes me jump. Dad joins me at the window and peers down. 'Ah, Finn has a bike,' Dad says admiringly. 'A Harley Davidson, isn't it? That's a classy bit of tackle.'

'He paid for it all himself. I wasn't keen. What mother would be?' Nola laughs as she says this.

We hear the thud of feet on the bare boards of the stairs. The door opens and a tall boy walks in. The first impression I get is of blackness. His hair is so dark it is nearly black and in the dimness of the room his eyes seem dark too. He is dressed in faded grey jeans and a black leather jacket, so old and pockmarked it could be the dark side of the moon.

'Hi,' he says to no one in particular. But I sense his eyes on me. And I am aware of my ugly cabbage green skirt and shapeless school shirt.

'Now,' Nola says triumphantly. 'Can you guess who this is?' Dad laughs. The boy moves closer, tugging off his jacket and throwing it over a chair as he does so. He looks at Dad and then glances back to me. I see then that his eyes are green, with raven lashes, and that his face is sharp boned and angular. He has sinewy arms and jutting shoulders. Everything about him is dark and sharp. I feel myself recoil from the frank appraisal in his eyes.

'Is it Rick who lived with us all those years ago? And if so—this must be the little princess!' He laughs then. It softens the taut lines of his face and he doesn't look so tough any more. I relax a little bit. He isn't so scary when he smiles.

'Now, where are those photographs of you two when you were babies?' Nola is saying.

'Oh no, please, Nola!' He is filling the kettle, making tea. He tries to grab the biscuit tin Nola has taken from the sideboard, but she moves away from him, laughing. Dad grins. I just watch them. I understand why he doesn't call her Mum or Mam—in some ways she seems younger than him.

'Don't be a spoilsport, Finn,' Nola says. 'You were sweet with Jade. You were lovely until you went to school and got contaminated.'

'Until I went to school and found out what a sissy you'd turned me into, you mean,' Finn says.

Dad and Nola laugh together. Dad seems really happy to be here with these people. I wish we could just go home. I don't want to see any photos. I will find something else to do for my art project. I'm certainly not coming back here again.

'Now,' Nola says, ushering me into a seat at the table. 'Just have a look at these.' She tips the tin full of photos on to the table and from the muddle of paper folders and loose prints selects one. It is a photo of a bundle in a blanket being held by Dad. He looks as if he's just won the lottery and I have to smile.

Dad squeezes my shoulder. 'You were two days old. I'd just brought you and your mum back from the maternity hospital. I drove all the way at twenty miles an hour. It felt like I had the crown jewels in the car with me.'

The boy sits down opposite me and watches unsmiling while Nola leafs through the prints. 'Now I must find the one of you two in the bath,' she says, her face crinkling with amusement.

'Oh no!' Finn says with a frown. 'Not that one!'

Nola and Dad seem to think it's funny that his face

is so stormy. They look at each other and grin. And Nola ferrets on until she proudly holds aloft a picture. 'Weren't they sweet?' she says to Dad and he nods. Nola hands the photo to me. I hold it out in front of me and study it.

It is definitely a photo of Finn. The same sharp cheekbones and radiant smile, this time in a child's face. He is sitting in a shallow bath of water carefully cradling a baby that is so small it could be a cheap doll. Behind him I can see parental hands and a smudgy face out of focus. This young Finn looks very pleased with himself.

Dad and Nola have taken a bundle of photos over to the window and are recounting stories of people I know nothing about.

I put the photo down on the table and avoid looking at the boy as I say dismissively, 'It's just silly. That's not a real baby! It's a toy.'

Finn's scowl becomes deeper, if that is possible. His dark eyebrows meet in an angry line. 'Never in the world,' he says. 'What would I be doing bathing with a dolly? It's you. Look, here's another when you learnt to sit up.' He leafs through the pictures and holds one out to me, I make no attempt to take it and he drops it on the table in front of me.

I stare down at the photographs, incredulous and slightly sick. 'Why on earth did they put me in the bath with you?' I ask in a whisper.

He gives me a look that is full of contempt. 'Because we were really hard up and it saved on hot water. Why else?'

I watch his bony white hands as he lays out mugs and biscuits. His skin is pale, milky white with a smattering of freckles, and it makes his eyes and hair seem darker. He hands me a scalding mug and I mutter my thanks. The tea is thick and bitter, nothing like the expensive tea we have at home, and there is no sugar to put in it, but I sip it anyway to give myself something to do.

Nola finds more photographs. Finn leans back in his chair, drinking his tea in gulps and scowling. I make a pretence of interest in the pictures. In most of them, thankfully, I am clothed. But even covered up I was without doubt the ugliest baby in the whole world. The young Finn presumably thought I was an alien; that is why he is always grinning and holding me as if I am a prize specimen. There are lots of pictures taken in the backyard on a hot day. Mum and Nola are wearing sun tops, Dad is bare-chested, and I am wearing a baggy towelling nappy. With my scrawny limbs and oversized head I look like ET's little sister. I keep staring at the younger Mum in the photos, who is holding me as if I am a Playdoh baby whose head might suddenly roll off, and wonder what was different about her.

'May I borrow this photograph?' I ask, holding up a ghastly shot of all of us bunched together with everyone grinning at the camera, everyone that is, except for me. I suppose I might be smiling but it's impossible to tell because I've got a large pink dummy in my mouth. I look like Sweetpea from the Popeye cartoons.

'I'm making a record of my life for my art project. It might be useful. I'll let you have it back.' I am asking more out of politeness than anything else.

'Finn's studying photography at college, he'll do some copies for you, if you like. He's got a dark room up in the attic,' Nola tells us. 'We are a nice little double act. I do the flowers for the weddings and he takes the photos. We're doing really well. And how about you, Rick? Still in the building trade?'

Dad pulls a face and shrugs his shoulders. 'By the skin of my teeth. I've had some good times and some very good times but things are a bit tough at the moment.'

'It's swings and roundabouts in business,' Nola says. 'I was all ready to pack in after Dad died. But then I realized they'd been making money out of the flowers. Not from people on the estate. Most of them are too busy making ends meet. But people from all over were ordering because Mam did arrangements so well and we delivered. So I finished with the fruit and veg. Things are so busy at the moment I'm going to have some help on a Saturday as soon as I can find someone suitable.'

To my amazement, and horror, Dad turns to me and says, 'There you are, Jade, just the thing for you. You've been desperate for a Saturday job for ages. See if Nola will take you on.' Turning back to Nola he says proudly, 'Jade's very artistic. She's doing art and design at school. She'd be great with flowers and things.'

Nola smiles at me and asks, 'Would you be interested, Jade? It's harder work than people think and you have to wrap up in winter because we don't have heating in the workroom. Flowers keep better in the cold.'

I swallow hard, trying to get my head around what is happening. It's true I've been on at my parents to let me work on Saturdays. Everyone else at school does and I feel a freak still relying on my parents for an allowance.

'Yes, great. I'd love to,' I say weakly.

'Well, try it for a couple of weeks and see how you feel,' Nola says kindly. 'Let's say three weeks trial, minimum wage and as much coffee as you can drink.'

'It's just transport . . . ' I say, suddenly hopeful that I can't take the job after all. 'We live right at the top of Thistle Hill. I'm not sure about the buses. I don't know how I can get here.'

'Oh, I'll drop you down,' Dad says cheerfully, as if we live down the road instead of at the other side of the city. 'What time do you want her to start, Nola?'

'Eight o'clock prompt start, finish at four, an hour for lunch.' Nola grins to lighten her businesslike tone.

'OK,' I say miserably. I duck away from Finn's cold stare and try to catch Dad's eye because I want to leave. I'm not even sure now I really do want to work on Saturdays instead of having a lie in and doing my homework at leisure. But I definitely know I don't want to work in a cold workroom on the St Aidan's estate.

I am quite cross with Dad when we get into the car, but he doesn't seem to notice. He just keeps on and on about how wonderful it is to have made contact with Nola and Finn again.

'If you were all such good friends I'm surprised you didn't bother to keep in touch,' I say a bit irritably.

'Yes, but we were all so busy. Life is frantic when you've got kids. And Nola was always on the move.'

'She seems pretty settled now,' I say. 'I hope she's going to be OK to work for. I don't know if I'll be any good with flowers.'

'Of course you will, Princess.' He spends the next ten minutes telling me how clever and wonderful I am. I am a little mollified but not totally.

Finally, puzzled by my surly mood, he adds, 'I thought you really wanted a job. You were on last week about going to Boots, on the cosmetic counter.'

I sit glumly and don't answer. He's quite right. I just think that in future I will be careful what I wish for. Sometimes wishes come true and not in a way you imagine.

Mum and Dad argue about my job. This is unbelievable. I honestly think it's the first time I've heard them have a proper row. I mean Dad always gets huffy when Mum throws out his old clothes and buys him new ones. He pretends to sulk for a bit but it soon blows over. Dad's funny. He's amazingly generous with us. I only have to so much as whisper I need something and he's rushing off with a cheque book, but quite mean with himself. Also he's colour blind and Mum says he has the dress sense of a tramp, so he and Mum are always spatting about ties that match and stuff like that. The only other time they have a tiff is when Nana is horrible to Mum and Dad tries to get her to stand up for herself. But all of these arguments are very low key.

But this time—this row—it's nasty.

Mum's face is quite pale with temper. 'It's not as if we need the money,' she says. 'And Jade's got her A levels.'

'Well, not for two years, she hasn't!' Dad says. 'Look, we're talking about her working Saturdays and finishing at four o'clock. Jack does evenings and weekends.'

'That's only because he wants to get out of the house and away from his mother.'

Dad sighs—you can't argue with the truth: 'It'll do the nipper good to get out into the world and meet people,' he says, trying to win Mum round with a smile.

'She should be studying,' Mum says, refusing to look at him.

'Let's ask Jadey what she thinks,' Dad says. He seems depressed by Mum's reaction. They both turn to look at me. I know how poor old Solomon felt when faced with those two mothers and one baby. What can I say to keep them both happy?

'I'm only doing a three week trial,' I say hopefully. Both their faces are stony. I try a different ploy. 'I think it will help me with my art,' I say, proud of myself for thinking up such a clever argument. 'I shall probably do some water colour studies in my lunch hour.'

Later in the kitchen, as I unpack my books, I see the photo in my school bag.

'Look what I've got,' I say to Mum. 'This will bring back some memories.' I hold out the rather crumpled photo that shows Nola with Finn on her lap, Mum holding me, and Dad standing with a pint of beer looking pleased with himself. Mum recoils as if it is a scorpion.

'There, wasn't I lovely?' I tease. 'I'm not surprised you haven't kept any photos of my early years. I was the most hideous baby ever born to womankind. Look, Mum, don't you want to see how beautiful I was?' I try to put the photo in her hand but she pulls away.

'There's something different about you,' I say, studying the print again.

'Sixteen years and a lot of wrinkles,' Mum says abruptly. 'Why have you brought it home, anyway?' she asks.

'I'm going to do a copy for my art. I know what it is!' I say suddenly, stabbing at the photo enthusiastically. 'Your hair was fair, it's quite blonde in this photo. Why do you dye it black? It suited you better like this.'

I look up into Mum's face. She has the strangest expression. This is how she looks when Nana has a go at her—tearful and hurt—as if the words have somehow bruised her soul.

'What is it, Mum?' I ask, concerned.

I see her swallow. She blinks a couple of times and smiles at me uncertainly. 'I went grey early. It's so ageing . . . I looked so washed out.'

'Maybe you should go blonde, then, for a change. I think you look lovely in this photo.' I put my arm around her shoulder and kiss her cheek. She seems so upset. I want to make her feel better. 'I promise if I get behind with my work or the job is too much I'll tell you.'

Mum pulls me into a hug and holds on to me really tightly, as if I might suddenly disappear and be lost to her forever. Her voice is husky as she says, 'You were the most beautiful baby in the world to us, we adored you.'

I feel really mean for teasing her. 'Yeah, of course I know that,' I say.

I don't have a chance to tell Jack about my trip to the St Aidan's estate and my job at *Flower Power* until we are walking down to Sybil's house. We take a short cut through the park and I tell him all about Nola and Finn.

'You don't sound very keen. Didn't you like them?' he asks gently, squeezing my hand.

'It was just so strange going there—they knew all about me and yet I didn't even know they existed. We must have been very poor when we lived there but my parents have never told me about it.'

'People want to forget the bad times, that's why,' he says reassuringly.

'They never talk to me about things. I think Dad is having trouble with his business but they still act as if I'm a little kid and whisper about it in corners.'

Jack shrugs. 'Better than taking pills and shouting at you all night. I know which I would prefer.'

I know Jack is referring to his mother and I feel awful complaining about my folks when he has such a terrible time at home. I squeeze his hand and find something cheerful to talk about.

Sybil lives in a huge terraced house near to the hospital. There's no front garden, just some iron railings and a drop down to the basement. You have to go up a flight of steps to get to the front door. Before we can ring the bell the door is flung open and there is Sybil, looking fabulous in a black leather micro skirt and glittery crop top. I feel a real freak in my jeans, training top, and baseball hat. I hadn't realized it was going to be a 'party' party.

Sybil is carrying a bottle of vodka and she waves it in welcome. We follow her inside. The house is full of noise and shouting. Just about everyone from school is here as well as loads of other people—there's hardly room to move.

The house is really weird—like stepping back into the past. The walls are covered in velvet paper that is lifting off at the edges and there are no carpets, just long faded rugs. The walls are covered with pictures: mostly gloomy oil paintings of landscapes or hunting scenes. There is a really horrible one of a saint being stoned to death. (I don't know how they live with it!) All the furniture is huge and dark and looks as if it should be in a museum.

'Come down to the kitchen and have a drink. Everyone is here and we're awash with booze. Come and get plastered!' Sybil yells.

The kitchen is quite small compared to the rest of the house. There's an old gas cooker in the corner and a big table completely covered with bottles and cans.

'It's just wild, isn't it?' Sybil says with satisfaction. 'I've never had a party like this before. I suppose this is what you get for being the most popular girl in the school.'

'And what do you get for being the most modest?' I ask. Sybil just laughs and flicks her hair back.

'Well, you have plenty to be modest about, Jadey! Joke!' she adds quickly and we all laugh as if this is really funny. Jack squeezes my hand.

After Sybil leaves Jack and I get a can of beer each and hang around in the kitchen. All the noise and shouting from the other rooms sounds a bit scary. I wander around the kitchen. On a notice board by the phone are photographs of Sybil when she was younger. She has long plaits and a sulky expression and is standing between two people who look like her grandparents. The woman has hair swept up in a bun and the man is balding with a beard and stooping shoulders—he looks as if he spends too much time reading.

Jack looks over my shoulder. 'Those are Sybil's parents. Her mother works at the Health Centre.'

'Blimey! They're old, aren't they?' I say and Jack nods.

From above us comes a loud crash that sounds suspiciously like a window being broken. 'I wonder if they know she's having a rave like this?' I say. 'The neighbours will be going mad.'

'I thought it was just going to be a gathering. You know, pizza and video,' Jack says gloomily.

Sybil comes whirling into the kitchen. 'Come on . . . ' she says to Jack. 'You can't spend all night hiding in here.

Jade, have some of this and lighten up!' she commands me, thrusting the vodka bottle into my hand. Then she dances out of the room with Jack trailing unwillingly behind her.

I sniff the bottle and take a tentative sip. It tastes horrible after the cool beer, hot and spiteful. It reminds me of Sybil. I wipe my mouth quickly with the back of my hand, wishing I hadn't bothered. I hang around the kitchen for a bit, looking out of the window. There's quite a large spooky back garden full of trees and bushes.

Lots of people I don't know come into the kitchen, talking and laughing. I wonder if they are gatecrashers or if Sybil has been into all the pubs in town and invited the world along to wreck her parents' home. Someone spills a bottle of red wine, but no one seems to care. The liquid lies under the kitchen table like a pool of blood. Depression grips me. I go looking for Jack.

The front room has been cleared of furniture and the music is thudding like a giant pulse. I peer through the darkness and smoke. My beer is now flat and warm and I am too hot in my training top. I want to go somewhere quiet like McDonald's and have a cool drink.

The music stops abruptly and a chorus of abuse is directed at the DJ. The crowd shifts as people go off in search of refreshment. And that's when I see Jack and Sybil.

They are standing together in the middle of the floor—seemingly oblivious to the fact that the music has stopped and no one is dancing. They're not dancing anyway—Jack is standing very tall and still, a blond statue, while Sybil winds herself around him like a glittery, leathery snake.

They are kissing so hard they are on Planet Snog and orbiting—lost in their own little world.

Then Jack pulls away and turns towards me. I can't bear to be caught standing and staring at them. I bolt from the room, barge through the crowds in the hall, and fall out of the front door.

A taxi has just pulled up at the kerb; through a blur of tears I see the couple from the photos getting out. Sybil's parents are home. They move towards the steps, staring up at the house with blank pale faces.

We cross on the bottom step and I hand the bottle of vodka to Sybil's mother. Then I am off down the road at a sprint. I know I ought to go to the taxi rank and get a cab home. But I can't face it. Tears are streaming down my face and my chest hurts from crying.

I dive into the gateway of the park, forgetting every lesson about stranger danger my mother drummed into me. The whole place is deserted, trees and bushes subdue the sounds of the city, and the thudding in my head is the sound of my own heartbeat.

When my shoulder is grabbed from behind I make a horrible strangled noise that passes for a scream: sure for a terrifying minute I have been stalked by a loony. Then I hear Jack's voice saying my name and the realization that he has followed me makes me weak with relief. I might have slumped down on to the path if he hadn't put his arms around me.

He pulls me close. 'Jade . . . Jade . . . I'm sorry.' He sounds absolutely broken. 'Please forgive me. I didn't mean to upset you.'

I pull away from him. He smells of drink and perfume. He smells of Sybil.

'Jade, please!' He looks close to tears. 'Jadey. I need a hug . . .'

This is our special code. 'I need a hug' means 'life's a bitch, I am feeling down, I need you to be my friend'.

Jack always needs hugs when he gets back from France. He needs hugs when his mum is upset and takes it out on him. He needs hugs whenever he is hurt. I have been giving him hugs since we were in reception class together. I am ace at hugs.

Wrapping my arms around his waist I press my hot face against his jacket. He is shivering even though the night is warm. I hate to feel him trembling—it's as if he's a frightened animal.

'I love you best in all the world, Jade,' he whispers. And I wonder why he sounds so sad as he says this. 'You are my best friend. You know that—don't you?'

'Yeah,' I say. 'We better get moving,' I add. And we start walking together through the darkness.

I think about the present Jack once brought me back from France. A pottery mug—it had 'I love you' on it, in French. I also have a whole collection of things with Bestest Friend on them that he has given me: key rings, pictures, pretend credit cards, birthday cards.

But he has never kissed me like he was kissing Sybil. I am confused and jealous. When the other girls at school talk about boyfriends and what they do together I just give my Mona Lisa smile and make jokes. I'd always believed that Jack and I would get around to all that kind of stuff one day—just not yet. Now I am not so sure.

'So what was going on with you and Sybil?' I ask eventually.

'She just wants to pull every boy in the school. She's just notching us up.' He sounds really bitter and angry.

'You could have said "no",' I suggest casually, as if I don't really care much one way or the other.

'I would have looked a complete prat,' he says miserably. 'I thought it would be a quick kiss and that was all. Jade, I promise you—I didn't want it—I didn't start it.'

'Well, it can't be much fun being treated like a sex object, can it?' I say bitterly. 'Not that I'd know much about it.'

'Jade!' He sounds really shocked. I pull away from him and start walking really fast, almost jogging. I can't help thinking how wonderful he and Sybil looked together. Like a fairy-tale couple—or the perfect people on the top of a wedding cake. What is the point of being Jack's best friend if he doesn't fancy me?

'Jade,' he has hold of my arm and is trying to turn me to face him. 'Please . . . ' he begs.

'I think I need a hug now,' I say, and my voice wobbles all over the place.

He kisses me then; it isn't the kind of kiss we normally share. This is a Sybil type kiss and I am startled and upset by it. I know Jack too well: I know when he is hurt or sad. I know when he is thinking about a story or a poem. I even know if he has a headache or gut ache. And I know now that he is desperate. I pull away.

'Let's go home. I'm tired,' I say quietly. And I turn away in case he sees the hurt and disappointment in my eyes.

He holds my hand very tightly, as if he is a little kid and I'm his mum and I might suddenly disappear. Maybe he's always been scared that his mother would run off like his father did. I want to comfort him, but I don't know how. I am hurting too much myself.

We walk to Jack's house and then I get a taxi home. Mum is sitting alone in the kitchen and her face is sombre. 'I thought you were going to ring when you wanted to come home?' she says, trying to smile.

'I didn't want to spoil your evening,' I say.

'That's sweet of you. It's not been much of a night. Your dad's had to go out.'

'Out? Again?' I exclaim.

'He's going through the books. There's a problem. Did you have a lovely time, darling?' she asks, with an attempt at brightness.

'It was OK,' I say, starting on the hot chocolate and biscuits she has placed in front of me.

'Oh—you had a bad time! You shouldn't have worn those old jeans and that scruffy top. Was everyone all dressed up?' Mum's eyes are round with concern.

I think about the loud music, the spilt wine, and the hot crowded rooms and sigh. What kind of a party did she think it was going to be?

Normally I tell Mum what is happening in my life. But I can't tell her about Jack and the failed kiss or the shock of seeing him and Sybil together. I spoon the froth from my hot chocolate into my mouth as if it is ice cream.

'How did you and Dad first meet?' I ask, desperate to change the subject.

'I was working in London as a nanny.'

'Was it love at first sight?' I question.

'Oh no! He'd had a heavy lunchtime session in the pub and was sleeping it off on a bench in the park. I thought he looked horrible. I had no intention of going anywhere near him. But as we were walking past little Felix dropped his ice-lolly and started screaming. That set baby Abigail off, so I had both of them grizzling. All the noise woke your dad and he was up quick as anything and rushing off to buy Felix another lolly.' Mum's face is soft as she remembers. 'He's never been able to bear the sound of a baby crying. It breaks him up. If you so much as whimpered in the night he was out of bed.'

'So what happened after he bought the lolly?' I ask.

'Well, I sat down on the bench with him and we got talking. After that we met every day when I took the children into the park. In no time at all we were married and had you.' Mum's face has flushed pink. She looks almost shy. 'Nana was . . . difficult to begin with. She thought he was rough. And he was really. But it wasn't his fault. But he and Grandad hit it off straight away. Grandad idolized him. Everyone does. He has a heart of gold.'

For some reason this story makes me feel really, really sad. I kiss Mum and take my hot chocolate up to bed. I don't like to think of Dad working late and Mum being here on her own. And I don't like to think of Sybil kissing Jack.

Sleep eludes me. I try thinking about my art project and cover the walls of the Tate and the National Gallery with my work before finally falling into a nightmare-riddled sleep. In my dreams the nearly naked saint from Sybil's house is chasing me through the park pleading with me to tend his wounds. I wake in the morning feeling exhausted. Next time insomnia strikes I will try counting sheep.

# 4

Saturday. The day I am to start work at *Flower Power*. I'm feeling so low; it's just what I don't need. The morning is damp and autumnal and below us the city is hung with heavy grey fog, like a film set for a Dickens novel. I imagine everyone down in the valley coughing and choking on pollution and the last thing in the world I want is to drive down there.

The silver birch trees Dad has planted in our garden have gold leaves among the green. It's the end of the year and for some reason this makes me feel really depressed. I don't want the summer to finish. I want to hang on to some remnant of my childhood. I want to go back to a life that revolved around summer holidays and Christmas. Back to a time when Jack was my bestest friend.

Mum and Dad are so gloomy and depressed you'd think I was having my last breakfast ever. Surely going out to work isn't as bad as all that? I am wearing my warmest trousers and a roll neck jumper, which happens to be black, which increases the funereal mood of the day. My tan is fading and black makes me look sallow and jaundiced. Not even washing my hair has made me feel better. I want to curl up in bed and sleep away the weekend until I see Jack again on Monday morning. Everything else in life seems a distraction.

Dad gets two phone calls during breakfast. Mum looks as if she's going to cry.

'Is everything all right?' I ask.

'I don't think it's anything your dad can't handle,' Mum says, but she doesn't sound very sure.

The city has a dreamlike quality as we drive through the centre. The tops of the buildings loom out of swirling banks of whiteness and the few people around are glimpsed as ghostly shadows.

The shop door at *Flower Power* is locked and we can't make anyone hear us. Dad knocks and rattles the letterbox and eventually Finn comes to the door and opens it. Despite the chill of the day he is wearing an old white T-shirt and faded denims. His black hair is ruffled as if he has just been pulling his fingers through it.

'We're very early. Sorry, did we get you out of bed?' I ask.

He gives me a dark look. 'I was up in the attic—developing some prints. Nola is out on a wedding delivery. You better come in.'

'Thanks,' I say. Dad raises his eyebrows at me and grins. Then he kisses me goodbye and tells me he will be back at four and if I need anything to ring him on his mobile. While all this is going on Finn is standing watching us, his arms folded against the cold morning air, his expression inscrutable.

As Dad pulls away Finn closes the door and locks it. 'First and most important lesson,' he says. 'Never ever leave the shop unattended unless you have locked the door first.' I feel unreasonably irritated that he feels I need to be told basic stuff like that.

'Fine,' I say. 'I know . . . this lot around here would steal fresh air.' I am only quoting Nola but it doesn't sound so clever coming from me.

'Do you want coffee?' he asks curtly.

'Only if you're having one,' I say. 'I don't want to be a nuisance. I'm sorry if we disturbed you.'

He yawns and doesn't reply. 'I didn't think you'd turn up,' he says, as he gets mugs and coffee out of the cupboard and switches the kettle on.

'Why?' I say, stung. 'I wouldn't have just not arrived.'

He shrugs his shoulders and stares unsmilingly at me. 'It's a bit of a come down for you, isn't it? Coming over from Thistle Hill to work here.'

He makes coffee and hands me a mug. It has a chip on the side. I wonder if he has given it to me on purpose. Out of the tail of my eye I watch him: aware of the muscles in his thin arms and the taut lines of his face. He's not the kind of person to get into an argument with. It would be easier to keep quiet but I can't help myself. I say tartly:

'I always try to keep my word. And anyway it's a job, isn't it?'

'There are lots of other places you could work. All the big department stores need Saturday staff,' he says. He has a disconcerting habit of staring at you as he speaks. I wonder if he does it to everyone. Or if I have been singled out for intimidation.

'Do they?' I say airily. I don't really see that it's any of his business.

'And it can't be that your parents want to do Nola a favour. They've never bothered with her over the years, not up until now, have they?'

'No,' I say, and then I add: 'I didn't even know you existed until this week.' As soon as I've said those words I know I've made a mistake. I chew at my lip as I watch his face. His jaw clenches and his green eyes darken like an angry sea.

'Yeah, well, we've managed fine without any of you up until now,' he says.

He begins to make toast. He moves with tight graceful movements. Even though I don't like him, and I know he doesn't like me, I find my eyes drawn to him. I watch his bony white hands and think about making a sketch of him. My caricatures are famous at school. I have a knack of picking out people's distinguishing features and turning them into a cartoon. Now I think about how I would turn Finn into a bony street fighter, with razor sharp cheekbones and knuckles like spikes.

'Do you want toast?' he asks.

I shake my head. My sketchbook is in my bag and I want to get it out and start drawing him. I find myself smiling as I think about it. Finn assumes I am smiling at him and gives me a puzzled look.

The shop door bangs, there are quick footsteps on the stairs and Nola breezes in. She is wearing an Afghan embroidered coat that would look awful on most people but looks amazing on her. I am suddenly shy with her. 'I'm ready to start work,' I say, finishing my coffee. 'I wasn't sure what to wear . . . '

'I'll give you an overall for the messy jobs.' She smiles at me. 'There's the workroom to tidy up and then you can open up the shop.' She is still talking to me as we clatter down the stairs. 'The workroom is always in a pickle. I go to the early market in Manchester and if I've got a wedding I start work as soon as I get back.'

Nola gives me a bin bag and I start to clear up the floor in the workroom. There are discarded flower heads among the broken stalks, leaves, and bits of wire. It seems a shame to throw buds and little roses away. I pick out the ones that are undamaged and heap them on the draining board. Then I wipe the tops down and sweep the floor.

Nola comes down to show me how to open up the shop. When she sees the flower heads she laughs. 'You're a natural, Jade. I can't bear to throw flowers away either.' She shows me how to make a Japanese arrangement where the flowers float in a bowl of water. It looks so good she suggests we put it in the window and I am flushed with success.

It's boring standing in the shop. The fog seems to have kept most people at home. I tidy up the greeting cards and then sneak my sketchbook out from my bag. I am itching to get started—once I have an idea in my head I am desperate to get it down on paper and see if I can make it work.

The sketch of Finn is amazing. I manage to get the way his hair grows in a spike in the front and the angular sharpness of his face. He has a very distinctive jaw line and a beautiful Roman nose. I lengthen his nose so he looks like Julius Caesar and make his eyes fierce and glittery. His mouth falls into a wonderful sneery smile. I make his body small with bulgy muscles like Popeye. And then I add his jacket: black and pockmarked, trailing gracefully from his hand like a pet snake. He looks really tough and rough. It's great! Absolutely the best thing I've ever done. I am astonished at how well I remember each and every tiny little detail of him. It's like he's been imprinted on my brain.

'What have you got there, sweetheart?' Nola's voice comes from behind my shoulder and makes me jump. I'd been lost in my drawing. I try to hide the sketch but she gives a crow of pleasure. 'Jade! That is wonderful! You are so talented. Let me have a look.' She takes the sketchbook from me, looks intently at the picture and bursts into a gale of laughter. 'Oh my goodness, wait until he sees this!'

'No!' My voice is loud with horror and embarrassment. 'It's not for him to see. Truly I wasn't going to show it to anyone. It's just for my art project.' My face is hot. 'Please give it back,' I beg, holding out a hand that isn't quite steady. I am terrified that Finn will come down the stairs before I get my book back.

'Only if you do one of me.' She moves into the centre of the shop and does a twirl.

'It would be easier if you had your coat on. It's so distinctive,' I say.

'Oh yes, yes. I love my coat. I bought it in Istanbul.' She's as excited as a child as she flips the book to me and races back upstairs.

She stands before me, looking eager, while I sketch her. The first one I do is very flattering.

'Oh no!' she says, looking at it. 'I don't want a whitewash job. I want one like Finn's.'

The next sketch I do makes her look zany. I exaggerate the curls, the cat-like eyes, and the embroidery on the coat. She looks like a hippie.

'Yes!' she shouts. 'Can I keep it? It's brilliant. Where did you get this amazing talent? Your mum could never draw a thing at school.' A spasm of anxiety crosses her face after she has said this, as if she might have offended me. 'You are a clever girl. Thank you,' she says quickly, and she kisses my cheek.

I carefully pull the sketch out of my book and hand it to her.

'Can I have the one of Finn as well?' she asks slyly.

'No!' Raw fear fills me. 'I'll do another one for you. But not that one.'

'Can I see the other sketches you've done? I love painting and drawing. I would have liked to have gone to Art College but I got pregnant with Finn when I was sixteen. Wow!' she says, as she looks at a page of sketches of Jack. They are not caricatures. They are true to life studies. I'm not very good at sketching but Jack has come out quite well. 'He's some looker,' Nola says in an awestruck voice. 'Is he your boyfriend?' she asks. I nod, blushing as I do so. It's not strictly true. But if he's not my boyfriend, what is he?

'He's actually my best friend,' I add more truthfully.

'Those are the best kinds of boyfriends to have,' she says with a grin.

We hear Finn coming down the stairs, his footsteps rapid and heavy. He marches into the shop.

'Before you go out, have a look at these. We've got a clever girl here. This is Jade's boyfriend. Handsome or what? And this is me.' She holds out the sketch I've given her.

'Yeah, great,' Finn says, glancing at it. 'It's very flattering, takes years off you,' he adds cryptically.

'Yours is the best, but she won't show it to you.' Nola giggles naughtily. 'Lads are so vain. It might break his heart to see himself as others see him,' she whispers to me.

'I don't know why you've been drawing me,' Finn says curtly, looking at me with narrow eyes.

'Because you're such an ugly mug,' Nola teases.

Then, before I can stop him, Finn reaches over, takes my sketchbook from my hand and flips it open.

'You have no right to do that,' I say furiously, trying to snatch it back. He stares down at the picture of himself.

'You have no right to draw me without my permission,' he says, throwing the sketchbook down as if it is trash.

'I can draw whatever I like!' I snap. 'Why can't your image be reproduced? Are you sacred or something?' I know I'm being impossibly rude but I am cornered and all I can do is attack.

Nola thinks it's hilarious that we are eyeball to eyeball scowling at each other. She goes off into a peal of laughter. 'Oh for goodness' sake, Finn. I think mine's brilliant. I'm going to have it framed. Don't be so po-faced.' Then she turns away, as if suddenly bored with us. 'Kiss and make up,' she adds. 'I've got work to do.'

She goes into the workshop. We stand in ugly silence, the sketchbook open on the counter in front of us. I drop my eyes first and it feels like a defeat. I close the book and turn away. He leaves without speaking, banging the door shut behind him, making the wind chime on the ceiling jangle and clank as if a hurricane had sped through the shop. A minute later I hear the roar of a motorbike engine and I try to feel relieved that he has gone. But I am filled with some kind of aching desolation and my eyes prickle with unshed tears. If I am not careful soon my whole world will be full of enemies.

He doesn't return and Nola is out for most of the day doing deliveries. I take quite a few telephone orders and serve a couple of customers. But it's not very exciting. I had no idea working in a shop could be so boring. I do a few sketches but the argument with Finn seems to have spoilt drawing for me and I can't concentrate. It's a relief when Mum and Dad arrive. I close up the shop and post the key through the letterbox as Nola instructed and walk away with a sense of relief.

As soon as I get into the Range Rover I know something is wrong. Dad is looking grim and Mum is wearing dark glasses and a Bardot-type headscarf as if the paparazzi are after her.

'What's the matter?' I ask.

'Daddy's business has been taken over by Sedgewick Coulson.'

'Is that good or bad?' I ask.

'We don't really know yet,' Mum says quickly.

'It's a very big company, Jade, it's the big league.' Dad sounds glum.

'Isn't it a compliment that they want Stevens and Co.? There must be lots of companies they could buy, surely?' I am puzzled now.

'We'll have to see,' Dad says. Then, in a very obvious attempt to change the subject, he says, 'I've talked to your mum about getting a rescue puppy and she's happy with the idea. So would you like to go to the kennels and see if there's anything that takes your fancy?'

'Oh yes!' I say joyfully. At last something nice has happened—the day is looking up.

At the animal rescue kennel we have to fill in loads of forms before we can go to see the dogs. Dad isn't his usual talkative self. The whole place seems to make him uncomfortable. I'm not surprised—the concrete floors are icy cold and the whole place stinks of disinfectant and dog pee.

Finally the helper smiles at us and says, 'That all seems to be in order. We have some lovely puppies, just ready to leave their mother. They have very pretty markings and should grow to medium size.'

'Oh, a puppy would be lovely. You can bond with it, Jade,' Mum says delightedly.

'I know the one I want if you've still got him. An Irish wolfhound cross that is nearly full-grown. My friend did a drawing of him when he came.'

'Oh . . . that will be Murphy.' The woman sounds uncertain. 'He's still here. But he's quite a handful. He really needs to go to a home that has knowledge of that breed.'

'My dad knows all about dogs,' I say quickly.

'Well—come and see him. He's in the end pen.'

We hear him before we see him. He seems to know he has visitors. The sound of his bark makes me shiver. The end pen has a nasty final ring to it. Murphy is standing up like a grizzly bear, with his paws up on the wire, howling into the roof. He is nearly as tall as I am and for a second I feel real fear.

'He's awfully big,' Mum says uncertainly. At the sound of her voice Murphy drops down and shoves his black nose through the wire, desperate for attention. He isn't at all beautiful. He has a huge head and skinny legs and looks more like a rough-coated grizzled lion than a dog. 'Just look at those paws,' Mum adds in an awestruck whisper. 'He's got a bit of growing to do yet.'

Dad is looking at the dog with a strange haunted expression on his face.

'Shall we just have a little look at the puppies . . . ?' Mum is saying. But Dad crouches down so his face is on a level with Murphy's.

'Hello, boy,' he says softly, and he puts his fingers through the wire so Murphy can lick them.

'He has got a very nice nature,' the helper says. 'He's just a bit boisterous. If it doesn't work out you can always bring him back to us. Unfortunately we do get a lot of dogs returned . . . '

'No!' Dad says sharply. Murphy is leaning against the wire trying to get closer to Dad and looking up at him with adoring brown eyes. Murphy's tongue is lolling—he looks as if he's smiling. 'If we take him—we keep him.' Dad turns to Mum and his eyes are very bright. 'He'll come round in time. You can see it in his face. He's a good 'un.'

'He's just so very big . . . ' Mum says weakly.

The helper gets a collar and lead. She goes into the pen with Murphy and he goes berserk, jumping all over her and licking her face and woofing as if he will eat her up.

Dad opens the door and marches in. 'Stop that!' he commands. Then he gets hold of Murphy by the scruff of the neck, shakes him down and says: 'SIT!' To our amazement Murphy does just that. Dad puts on the collar and lead and strokes Murphy's ears. 'There's a good lad,' he says and his voice is gruff with love.

'Well that's a good beginning. He seems to know who the boss is,' the helper says.

Dad may have won a battle but there is still a war raging. Murphy leaves the dogs' home at a gallop with Dad fighting for control and Mum and I running behind. Then, when we reach the Range Rover, Murphy refuses to get in. He pulls away like a wild pony and whines.

'He thinks it's the Dog Warden's van,' Dad says sadly. 'He's got no trust.'

Finally Dad lifts Murphy in and he settles down on my lap. It's like being cuddled by the biggest teddy bear in the world.

'Don't let him lick your face,' Mum says anxiously. 'He's probably got worms. I do hope he hasn't got fleas,' she adds. 'Are you all right under there, Jadey?'

My voice is muffled as I reply. 'He needs a bath—he stinks of the dogs' home. It's vile.'

'It's Jeyes fluid,' Dad says. 'Nasty stuff. We used to have something similar painted on our heads when we were kids to get rid of the nits. Wonder it didn't fry our brains. Probably did—but no one cared.'

I wish they would stop talking about fleas and nits. I'm itching all over.

When we get home I phone Jack and he comes around immediately. We let Murphy out into the garden and he goes crackers. At first we have to stand guard to make sure he doesn't leap over the hedge. Then he runs round and round in circles and Jack and I dance about the garden together throwing sticks for him. It's brilliant because Jack is all lit up and happy.

While Mum is cooking supper we bath Murphy. We all get absolutely soaked but Murphy smells loads better because we use Mum's Badedas on him as we don't have any dog shampoo.

We are having salmon for supper but Mum gets a joint of beef from the freezer and cooks it in the microwave for Murphy. 'Lots of vegetables and no salt, just like for a baby,' she says with satisfaction.

Murphy gulps down his food as if he fears it might be stolen before he finishes it. Then he stretches out on the rug before the Aga and feigns sleep. I know he is only pretending because he keeps on opening one eye to look at us. I expect he's scared it's all a dream and if he goes to sleep we will disappear and he will be back in his pen at the dogs' home.

Supper is great—like a party. Mum and Dad aren't miserable any more. They don't mention Dad's business or the takeover and the phone doesn't ring. (Miracle!) We drink to Murphy's health in sparkling wine.

'This is like his birthday. We will have to celebrate it every year!' I say. And we play a silly game called 'Dog's Party' when we think of games and food dogs would like to have.

Jack and I take Murphy into the garden for his last run. A cold northern wind has swept the fog away. The sky is clear and scattered with stars. High in the sky a huge moon hangs like a Chinese lantern.

Murphy, weighed down by beef and veg, snuffles in the flowerbeds and lopes about. Jack and I hold hands and look up at the sky. In the moonlight Jack's face is very sculpted and beautiful. I wonder if he is writing a song in his head. He is miles away—deep in thought—not with me at all. But I don't care. I want life to stay like this forever. I want to capture this moment and hold on to it for all time.

He turns to me: 'Jade . . . There's something I need to tell you . . . '

'Cooee, Jade. Phone!' It's Mum, at the door of the conservatory, holding my mobile out to me. Cursing silently (princesses don't swear) I jog over and grab the phone.

'Hi! It's Sybil.'

'Hi . . . ' My heart sinks. I have a sudden cold premonition of trouble ahead.

'My parents are really sorry about last night. You being invited here and then those gatecrashers turning up. I was really scared but the police came and got rid of all those horrible people.' Sybil is lisping down the phone to me as if she's about six.

'It's OK.'

'My parents want you and Jack to come and have supper with us, to make up for last night. How about tomorrow? About six? See you then. Byee!'

She doesn't give me a chance to say no or argue. I am stunned by her cheek.

'Sybil wants us to go to her house for supper, tomorrow,' I tell Jack.

'Oh hell,' he says.

'She didn't give me a chance to say no.'

We trail into the house. I want to ask what he was going to tell me before Sybil interrupted us. I have a gut feeling it was something important. But the moment seems to have passed.

Any idea I have of phoning Sybil back and making an excuse is killed stone dead by Mum and Dad's insistence that it would be wrong to refuse to go.

'It would look so rude, Jade,' Mum says. 'After all

Sybil has been for supper here. You only have to go for an hour or two.'

Jack's eyes meet mine across the table and we smile at each other. I suddenly feel happy and strong and confident. Nothing can come between us. He's told me he loves me and I am his best friend. What more do I need?

# 5

Murphy won't sleep on his own. That's the first problem. He scratches and claws at the utility room door and howls into the night as if he is being eaten alive by wolves.

Dad goes backwards and forwards to try to calm him down. In the end Dad brings Murphy upstairs. I pad out on to the landing to find out what is going on. Dad is asking Mum to let Murphy sleep in their room.

'We won't make him feel secure by making him insecure. He thinks when we're out of sight we've gone for good,' Dad explains.

I don't think Mum is really interested in dog psychology at the moment. She turns away, muttering: 'Well, he's not coming on the bed.' I can almost hear her thinking how nice and easy a little puppy would have been. 'I hope we're not going to have this every night,' she adds.

'He'll soon settle down,' Dad says encouragingly. 'Won't you, my old son?' he says, stroking the top of Murphy's head. And Murphy looks up at Dad with adoring brown eyes, as if Dad has just flown down from heaven to save him. Everyone, especially Murphy, seems to have forgotten he was meant to be my puppy.

In the morning I sneak into their room to see what has happened. Murphy is lying on Dad's dressing gown on the floor next to Dad's side of the bed. He has his nose inside Dad's slipper. It makes me realize that adoration can have a down side. (Because if I am absolutely honest I do not want to share my dressing gown with Murphy.)

I try all sorts of ways to get out of going to Sybil's house for supper. In the end I say to Mum that maybe I ought to stay in and look after Murphy. But she looks anxious and says, 'Sybil's mother will be expecting you. She will have all the food ready. You can't cancel it now, Jade. It would be so rude.'

So Jack and I walk down to Sybil's house. And—guess what?—Sybil's mother has completely forgotten we were coming! And Sybil, being the caring, thoughtful kind of person she is, hadn't bothered to remind her. I think of all the effort my mum makes when friends come to the house and I am really cross.

They can't even pretend they haven't forgotten because the kitchen table is set for three people and they are already eating their meal. The walk through the park has made me quite hungry and I stare down at the food with a growing sense of unease.

Sybil gets some more plates and cutlery and puts them down on the table. Nothing matches and they don't have a proper tablecloth just a plastic one. It's as thin and wrinkly as an ASDA carrier bag and so old the rose pattern has almost rubbed away. Sybil has this really catty smile on her face. Her mother is checking their diary to see if it's our mistake or hers.

'It doesn't really matter,' Sybil's mother says, on finding it's her mistake. I bet she wouldn't say that if we had turned up on the wrong evening. 'There's plenty of food,' she adds. 'We're having lentil burgers, couscous, bulgar and mixed bean salad—very nutritious.'

Sybil's father is eating a bowl of nuts. He doesn't take much notice of us.

'Help yourselves,' Sybil's mother says. I decide to be polite and try loads of everything.

As soon as I start eating I realize I have made a big mistake. It is all incredibly filling and after a couple of mouthfuls I am completely stuffed. Dismay engulfs me as I try moving the food to the edge of the plate and back into the middle again—but it doesn't look any less. In fact spread out it looks even more. The huge red beans in the salad gleam up at me like evil eyes. I count how many I've still got to eat and try not to shudder.

'Do you get given vegetarian food at home?' Sybil's mother asks me rather pointedly.

I am chewing a bean very slowly. I swallow hastily. 'Yes, we have vegetable lasagna, with aubergines. It's one of my favourites.'

'Very fatty,' Sybil's mother says. 'Aubergines absorb a great deal of oil. Best avoided. My husband is a vegan. We don't have cheese sauces.' She says this as if cheese sauces are the height of decadence.

After that we sit in silence apart from the sound of chewing. I know now how cows feel when they are working their way through the cud. I could do with four stomachs, or at least one a bit bigger than my own. In the end I admit defeat. Jack has heroically cleared his plate. Maybe he was clever and took less than me.

'If you aren't used to vegan food you'd better have a cup of peppermint tea,' Sybil's mother says. 'It will help to get rid of the gas.' The expression on Jack's face makes me want to giggle.

'Shall we go to the cinema?' Sybil suggests. 'If we leave now we'll be in time for *Stargazer.*'

I stare at her for a moment. I have a horrid feeling this is all part of her plan and I have been set up in some way. Her mother agrees reluctantly. Her father is still eating, spooning bulgar into his mouth very slowly.

'My husband chews everything fifty times before swallowing,' Sybil's mother explains, as if noticing me staring. 'Most of us abuse our digestive systems,' she adds.

Jack and I smile politely. My head is going up and down like a nodding dog in the back of a Ford Fiesta. I want so much to get out of Sybil's house I have a stress pain in the pit of my stomach—or maybe it's the beans starting their beastly business with my insides?

When we get to the multiplex we find most of the school is there too. Sunday evening is a really popular time to go to the cinema. Loads of people who were at the party cut Sybil dead. But there is a big gang of year elevens, including Nicola Holden, Lucy's sister, who scream: 'Hi, Sybil!' and mob her as if she's a film star. Any minute I expect them to ask for autographs.

Sybil fights off her fan club and goes off to buy sweets. She comes back with a box of Jelly Babies. When she offers them to me I shake my head. I might explode if anything, even a Jelly Baby, reached my stomach. I feel like an over-inflated bike tyre.

Sybil stuffs her mouth full and then she starts this really silly game with Jack, feeding him Jelly Babies like he's a little kiddy. She's showing off because Nicola Holden and her gang are standing close by and watching us. (We ought to charge them.)

'Here's a black one, open wide,' Sybil says, leaning up against Jack and staring into his eyes. When he doesn't open his mouth quickly enough she rubs the Jelly Baby against his bottom lip.

'And now a little yellow one,' she giggles, and I am sure I hear Nicola Holden giggle too. I don't understand why Jack just stands there and lets her do it. He looks a fool, but not such a fool as me.

'Maybe I will have one after all,' I say lamely, holding out my hand, but Sybil ignores me. Jack looks hypnotized like a rabbit caught in headlights. He doesn't even seem to know I am here.

'Thanks, Sybil,' I say loudly. The giggles from Nicola Holden are clearly audible now. I feel my face heating from anger and humiliation.

'And now a little baby, a little baby pinky one,' Sybil is saying in a soppy voice. She places the red Jelly Baby in her own mouth as if it is a cig butt and leans up to Jack, waiting for him to bend, like a baby bird, and take it from her mouth.

Anger hits me like a wave of seasickness, my legs feel weak and my heart is beating too fast. I never realized before how highly toxic pure rage could be. I try to reach out my hand to grab Sybil's shoulder but I am unfocused and shaking.

'Hello, Jade. How you doing?'

We all turn—I see it happening as if in slow motion. Jack, glazed eyed, with a sheen of sweat on his upper lip. And Sybil, with the red Jelly Baby disappearing into her own mouth with a soundless plop.

'Hello, Finn . . . ' I whisper. I feel a pain in my side as if my heart is being cut. My whole body is throbbing with agony. Why, of all the people in the world, did he have to be here? Because I know as I look into his eyes that he had been watching us and seen what was happening. For a crazy moment I wonder if I am being paid back for humiliating him with the cartoon. It seems like some kind of justice that he should be here to see me being made a fool of.

He's dressed all in black and his hair is swept back from his bony forehead. In his beaten-up old jacket with his sharp, pale face he looks dark, dangerous, and grown-up.

'Hi!' Sybil barges me out of the way and holds out the box of sweets. 'Do you want a Jelly Baby?' she purrs, swinging her hips and smiling at Finn.

I wait for his reaction but there isn't one.

'No thanks,' he says, and he doesn't even glance at her. He is looking at me—looking straight into my eyes. 'I should eat them up yourself,' he adds dismissively, as if she is an irritating child.

'What are you going to see?' he asks me, and he moves nearer, effectively blocking off my view of Jack and Sybil. I'm quite relieved. I don't know which of them I am more angry with. I suppose I ought to be grateful to Finn for arriving in the nick of time and stopping me from making a complete idiot of myself, but I can't find any good emotions inside me any more. My head is full of rage and despair and to my shame I mutter my reply like a sulky child.

'*Stargazer*—Screen 4. What about you?'

'I don't know yet. I came down with some mates. *Stargazer* sounds good,' he adds softly. I wonder why he is bothering to be nice to me. There is a film on about a motorbike gang showing on Screen 3—surely that would be more in his line?

'Yeah, I think it'll be good.' I flap my ticket and wish the pain in my heart and the ache in my gut would go away.

'Maybe I'll join you—would that be OK?' he asks. His green eyes are narrow, watching my face intently. I try not to look surprised. I've done nothing to deserve his kindness.

'Yeah,' I say again.

'Are you OK? Is there anything I can get you—a drink or an ice cream?' His voice is concerned and those inky eyebrows of his are pulled together in a little frown. He's talking to me like he's my uncle or something.

'Some peppermints would be nice,' I whisper.

'Come on, then,' he says. 'See you around,' he says to Jack and Sybil and the tone in his voice is a real brush off. Then he takes hold of my hand and leads me off to the sweet counter like I'm a little kid.

I'm completely wiped out with pain. First there's the hurt from realizing that a lifetime of devotion to Jack has just ended. And then there is the terrible agony in my stomach.

'Are you sure that you're OK?' Finn asks when the film starts. I am doubled over by this time.

'Yeah, fine,' I lie (like I always sit as if I'm the Hunchback of Notre-Dame).

I don't have a clue what the film is about. I am taken

up with watching Sybil and Jack who are sitting a couple of rows in front of us. Sybil spends the entire film leaning over Jack and whispering.

Rage boils around in my head. I am furious with Jack. I keep thinking about all the kindness my parents have shown to him. I remember how I got into trouble for fighting at Junior School because if anyone hurt Jack I would have a go at them, lashing out with sharp words and sarcasm. I have never wavered in my love and friendship. So how, after all these years of being best friends, can he treat me like this? I am also angry that he has dumped me for Sybil. He must be really stupid to have fallen for someone so obvious. And it hurts that for all these years I've been in love with someone who is a dumbhead.

The only little crumb of comfort I have is that Finn cut Sybil dead like she was some old washerwoman. I bet not many boys do that to her. It warms my feelings towards him. When he takes hold of my hand I don't pull away. In fact I feel so lonely and miserable I lean against his shoulder and get some comfort from the warmth and nearness of him. I feel as sad and unloved as a stray cat. Rage gives way to despair and I feel really sorry for myself.

At the end of the film when we are all filing out Jack comes and finds me. His face is as white as paper.

'Jade,' he says desperately. I try to sidestep him. But he moves in front of me. Apart from knocking him over there's no way of getting past him. 'Jade. How are you getting home?' he asks anxiously.

'I'm going on the back of Finn's motorbike,' I say with cavalier abandon.

Jack looks horrified. 'I don't think your mother . . . ' he starts to say.

'Oh, drop dead,' I say. Jack glances at Finn's stormy face and makes his way back to Sybil's side. She's busy shrieking at Nicola Holden and her friends.

'Wasn't it a super film? Did you cry? I sobbed all the way through. It was soooo sad!'

When Finn and I get out to the car park he says, 'I would take you on my bike. You'd be quite safe. I've got a spare helmet in the box, but you'll be very cold even in my jacket.'

'It's OK,' I say wearily. 'My mother would have a nervous breakdown if I arrived home on a motorbike. She fusses when I go out on a push-bike. I'll ring my dad and he'll come for me. You don't have to wait. I'll go back inside when Jack and Sybil have left. It's cold out here.'

'I'll stay with you,' he says gruffly.

I'm too miserable to make conversation. We stand in silence. My teeth start to chatter.

'Are you sure you don't want to go inside?' he asks.

'No, my dad will be here in a minute,' I say. I am actually too miserable to move. I can't bear to go back into the lights of the cinema. I want to stay out here in the cold dark and nurse my pain.

I think how nice it was when Finn held my hand and I would quite like to move closer to him and snuggle inside his jacket with him. But he seems distant and grown-up now we are outside the safe intimacy of the cinema.

Through the gloom I see Dad's Range Rover arrive in the entrance of the car park. 'Thanks very much,' I say.

'Why? I didn't do anything.' He sounds almost annoyed, as if I shouldn't be thanking him.

'You got me the peppermints.' Then some kind of crazy impulse moves me. I think it's because he's the only person who's been decent to me this evening. I move forward and try to kiss him on the cheek. I have to stand on tiptoe because he is so much taller than me. I get the corner of his mouth before I connect with the slight roughness of his face and this embarrasses the hell out of me. He doesn't make any move to kiss me back. 'See you Saturday,' I say quickly.

He doesn't reply. I feel a complete fool. My face is burning as I walk across the car park and get into Dad's car.

'Who was that?' Dad asks.

'Finn Casey.'

'What happened to Jack and Sybil?'

'They went back to Sybil's house.'

'Didn't you want to go with them?'

'No!'

'Oh, like that is it?' Dad says. 'Have you fallen out with them?'

I don't reply. My parents live in some kind of time warp. In their minds I am still ten going on eleven and squabbles with your friends are over silly little things and in no time at all you are all chanting 'Make friends, make friends, never never break friends'. I wonder for a moment what Dad would say if I told him the truth.

My mobile keeps on ringing. I don't answer it and when I check the number I find it is Jack. I don't want to talk to him. I don't want to hear any more excuses.

'Sybil's mother has poisoned me!' I announce dramatically to Mum when I get home. I describe in graphic detail the ghastly food we had.

'It's only wind. You were always a very colicky baby—we hardly had a wink of sleep in your first year. What you need is some gripe water,' Mum says. Then she adds with a worried frown, 'I do hope Sybil's mother cooked those beans properly. They can be poisonous if they're not boiled for long enough. I suppose a doctor would know about that sort of thing,' she adds, but she sounds a bit doubtful. Mum fusses around me and sends Dad out to the late night store for a bottle of gripe water.

Mum gives me six spoonfuls straight from the bottle.

'Beans, beans, good for the heart. The more you eat, the more you—' Dad starts saying.

'Shut up, Rick,' Mum says sharply. 'It's not funny.

Jadey's in pain. Horses die from colic,' she adds. (That cheers me up no end.)

I am a bit worried that Dad will tell Mum I've had a falling-out with Jack and I will have to talk to her about it. I know Mum will see straight through any brave words and if I start to cry I may never stop. So I go upstairs, have a bath, and get into bed.

But as soon as I get under the duvet the pain gets worse. In my mind I see those big kidney-shaped beans again. And then I get to thinking that I didn't chew them well enough and now, maybe, one has lodged in my appendix. Nana always goes on about not eating apple pips or anything that might 'get caught up in your insides'. Goodness knows what Nana would say about those beans with their pasty white filling and tough inedible skins. Something along the lines of 'not fit for pigs', I'm pretty sure.

I creep out of bed and wander downstairs with my arms crossed over my aching stomach. I feel sorry for myself and am hoping Mum will give me the rest of the gripe water or make me a hot-water bottle. I feel so ill I would like her to sit next to the bed and hold my hand for a bit. I can hear the buzz of voices in the kitchen. Mum and Dad are talking quickly and urgently.

'You know what a blabbermouth Nola's always been. She can't keep anything to herself.' Mum doesn't sound angry, just rather tired and worn out. 'It would be better for us to tell her, Rick.'

'No!' Dad sounds really upset, tearful even. 'There's no reason to think Nola will say anything.'

'What about Finn? What if he knows? Is Jade getting friendly with him?'

'It looked to me like they were having a bit of a kiss and cuddle,' Dad says miserably.

'Kissing!' Mum says in an outraged tone.

'She is sixteen,' Dad says. 'I suppose she's nearly grown-up . . . '

'That's why she needs to be told. It's only fair, Rick, and it would be awful if she found out from someone other than us.'

'No!' Dad says again. 'I can't face it.'

'Well, you were the person who took her down to Nola's!' Mum sounds upset now. 'Why couldn't you have left well alone?'

'Our baby asked to go there. I didn't think. I can't face telling her. Please don't make me tell her. It'll break my heart. It's on the cards that I'll lose the business, I can't face losing her too . . . ' Dad is crying now, I'm sure of it.

I have to restrain my impulse to burst into the kitchen and throw my arms around him. It hurts me deep inside to hear him sobbing.

'Maybe we should have told her when she was little, so she would always have grown up knowing.' Mum's voice is full of sadness.

'Oh no . . . no . . . ' Dad says. And then there is silence; the only sound is Murphy whimpering, as if the broken note in Dad's voice has upset him too. I hope Mum has her arms around Dad and is giving him a hug. He really sounds as if he needs one.

Stealthily I make my way back up the stairs. The shock of eavesdropping has cured my stomach pains. Or maybe the rest of me is hurting so much I just can't feel them any more.

Getting into bed I try to absorb what I have heard. Nola, and possibly Finn, know a secret about me. Something which Mum thinks I need to know and which upsets Dad to talk about. How could he possibly lose me? What could they have to tell me that would be bad enough to kill all the love between us?

I've always thought I really appreciated my parents. From being really small I've had the example of Jack's to compare them with and my parents have always won hands down. But up until now I've never realized just how much they really mean to me.

I try to think of what the secret could be—this terrible thing I have not been told. Maybe Dad has been in prison? If so it must have been a long time ago. And so what? He's always been good to me. In fact when I think about it he's always been good to everyone. He is brimming over with generosity and kindness. He can't walk past a beggar in the street without emptying his pockets. If he did do something bad in his early life it would definitely have been a mistake and not a case of deliberate wickedness. I know that for sure. And I know that nothing could change the way I feel about him.

Into my mind slips the word I have been trying not to think about—ADOPTION. Maybe I am adopted. Nana's words come back to haunt me. 'Who does she take after?'

I lie in bed, staring into the darkness, trying to get my head round the idea that my parents might not really be my parents. Is this why Mum dyes her hair? So she will look more like me?

One of the little girls I was best friends with at Junior School was adopted and Mum used to talk to me about it. 'Juliet is very special—she was chosen by her mummy and daddy,' Mum would say and I was actually quite envious. Being chosen sounded really exciting. I had visions of lots of babies in cots and Juliet's mother and father walking along the rows looking down at each one—like people do with the furniture at IKEA. And then maybe her mother saying, 'Oh, do look at this one, isn't she sweet? We must have this little one with the golden curls. I've fallen in love with her.' When I was six that whole scenario appeared a lot more glamorous than being planted like a seed, growing in your mother's tummy for nine months, and then just popping out.

So if I was adopted why didn't they just tell me then that I was chosen? But there again, who would willingly choose a baby who looked like an alien and had chronic wind for the first year of its life?

Hot tears of self-pity well up and trickle down my cheeks. I want to hang on to being Dad and Mum's little princess. I don't want anything to ever change that.

# 6

For the first time in my life I am nervous and unhappy at the thought of seeing Jack. Part of me wants to talk to him about the conversation I have overheard. I am used to sharing all my problems with him. But part of me is so sore and hurt that I dread the idea of talking to him or anyone else about what I have discovered.

On the way to school he sends me a text message. We are meant to go to a whole school assembly on Monday mornings but he asks me to meet him in the common room kitchen and skip assembly. This is a high risk strategy because Big Willie places great store by us all turning up for our act of collective worship. On the other hand no one but the sixth form are allowed to use our kitchen. We even have to clean it ourselves, so it's a pretty safe place to hide away in.

'C U in the broom cupboard!' I text back to him.

It's a bit difficult walking against the tide of people but I manage to dodge into the kitchen and hide from sight until the school settles into unnatural stillness. Just faintly, in the background, can be heard the reedy note of voices singing 'Fight the Good Fight': the sound shivers through the morning air like far off bird song. I hold my breath and wish my heart wasn't thudding so hard. The door opens and Jack slips in. He is breathless and his hair falls in a golden lock over his forehead.

We don't speak for a moment. We just look at each other. His blue eyes are troubled and his mouth curves sadly. He is so beautiful and I love him so much I want to cry. Then I see his chin tremble. He whispers my name and holds out his arms to me. I walk into them. He hugs me close and then I really am crying. I think he might be crying too. And we are both whispering at the same time. Our breathless words pile on top of each other like falling snowflakes in a blizzard. My words are angry and fast—his are slow and soft. Finally I finish telling him what a creep he is and how much I hate Sybil. My anger fades and I shut up and listen to him.

'Oh, Jade.' He presses his face against my damp cheek. His voice is shaking. 'Please forgive me. I love you so much. If I didn't have you I don't know what I'd do. I couldn't go on without you, you know that, don't you?'

I don't like to hear him talk like this. I know he gets really depressed, but he sounds as if he is ready to throw himself under a bus at any moment. I soothe him, stroking his hair with my hands. 'It's all right, Jack. I'll never let you down. I'll always be here for you,' I promise, and I really mean it. I am scared to think of what might happen to us if we split for good.

'One more chance—that's all I ask . . . ' he says.

He kisses my cheek, nuzzling at me like a kitten with its mother. 'I wrote a song last night,' he says. 'I'll sing it to you, if you like.'

'OK.' I relax into his arms, holding him tight, letting the warmth and nearness of him soothe me. We are wrapped together in a gorgeous cuddle and he is whispering this lovely melody in my ear when the door creaks. It slides open so slowly we assume it is the draught and nothing more. Then this voice intrudes into our little pool of love and warmth like an air raid siren.

'Jade Stevens and Jack Lavelle. What on earth are you up to? You should be in assembly not in here . . . doing . . . doing whatever it is you are doing.' It's The Frog. Her face is all red and screwed up and she is blinking too fast. In her hand is a jug. She has obviously come in here to nick our milk allocation. No wonder we are all on black coffee by mid morning if the staff just come in and help themselves. We all put money in a kitty to buy milk, coffee, and tea, so she has absolutely no right to come in here for freebies.

I open my mouth to tell her this but Jack squeezes my hand warningly, as if reading my mind.

'And stop holding hands,' The Frog snaps. 'Go and wait outside Mrs Williams's office.'

'Yes, Miss Froggit. By the way, would you like some milk before you go?' I add, and she gives me a look worthy of a viper.

'Why did you mention the milk?' Jack asks miserably, as we stand in the corridor outside Big Willie's door. 'It won't help.'

'Honestly, it's the first time I've ever broken a school rule or done anything wrong and I get caught by that old moo creeping around nicking our milk ration. It's just too sickening. Why can't she stay in the staffroom where she belongs?'

'Just calm down, Jade.' He slips his arm around me. Unfortunately at that exact moment Mrs Williams opens her door.

'I really didn't need Miss Froggit's graphic descriptions. I think I can see quite clearly what the problem is for myself,' she says with heavy sarcasm. 'Come in, both of you. And stand well apart,' she adds, as if we are combustible. 'Now,' she breathes heavily, snorting out through her nose as if she is an asthmatic pig. 'It grieves me to have to caution you two. You both have excellent records and are form prefects.' She huffs again. 'But,' she pauses ominously, 'but school rules are quite clear. No outward show of affection between students of the opposite sex.'

For about the first time in my life I answer back to a teacher. 'I suppose if we were the same sex that would be all right,' I mutter. Jack looks astonished and stares at the floor.

Big Willie ignores me—she is talking to some point in the carpet midway between us. 'There is not only the fact of missing school assembly but you were hiding in the kitchen indulging in inappropriate behaviour.'

'Mrs Williams,' I interrupt, 'we were talking when Miss Froggit came in—and that was all!'

'I am not interested in semantics, thank you, Jade,' Big Willie says. Her eyes are small and mean. Sometimes, when she is benign, she reminds me of a nice old whale, but now she is more like a shark, a huge killer, scenting blood and looking for prey.

'You will receive a bad conduct ticket and a letter will go home to your parents. I have the reputation of the school to consider,' she adds nastily.

End of interview. End of my school career as teachers' pet and model pupil. And the awful thing is I really don't care. I march through the school and when Sybil comes near to me I snarl at her, 'Just eff off and keep away from me and Jack!'

Nana (the professional gloom-monger) says deaths, troubles, and debts always come in threes. Certainly today trouble is coming thick and fast for me. First lesson is Art. I have to try to explain to Mr Garforth, the teacher, why my portfolio is nearly empty and I have virtually nothing to show on my childhood project.

'It's half term next week and the deadline is the week after,' he says ominously. 'You do know why it is called a deadline—don't you, Jade?' I suspect this is an attempt at teacher-type-humour so I just smile and nod.

Everyone else has masses of work and I sense Mr Garforth's eyes on me as I scratch away at a copy of the photo I borrowed from Nola. I can see that if I am not careful I will be getting another bad conduct ticket. If you get three there's a full staff review on you. I sense the short slippery slope from being a good student to being a suitable case for expulsion lying before me like a trap. Yet I haven't set out to do anything wrong. (What is it that

Nana is always saying—'The road to ruin is paved with good intentions'—oh, hell!) I wish Nana's voice would get out of my head and leave me alone. She kind of haunts me when things go wrong, a gruesome old banshee looming over my shoulder, wailing out predictions of disaster. The awful thing is she is so often right. Today I can see that success and failure are separated by very little.

Dad says this about people who end up sleeping on the streets. 'It happens so easily, it's frightening,' he said to me once when I pointed out it was a waste to give money to beggars. 'You lose your job, you can't pay your rent, your giro doesn't arrive, and there you are—dossing in a doorway. And there ain't no bank managers begging to give you a loan then.' This is why he won't walk past a homeless person—even if he knows they will spend the money he gives them on cider or worse. 'There but for the grace of God . . .' Dad always says.

Now I think about the troublemakers in the school who have been sent off to special units and labelled as no-hopers. And I realize that it could happen to any of us. Any time. As Dad says—it's just so easy . . . It's almost as if I can see my fall from grace happening before my eyes. I decide I must act. Mum and Dad deserve better than this.

Trouble number three arrives after school. (Just like Nana could have predicted!) Jack and I walk down to meet Mum and the most terrible sight meets our eyes. The inside of the Range Rover has been ripped to pieces. It looks as if a group of thugs with flick knives have had a go at it. Mum's eyes are all red and swollen from crying. Murphy is stretched across the back seat looking bemused. There're bits of foam and plastic in his coat especially around his muzzle.

'You'll both have to sit in the back. He's chewed through the front seat belt,' Mum says in a trembling voice.

'Why? How?' I ask.

'Dad's gone down to London to a special meeting with the company who've bought his business. I thought I'd go to the pet superstore and get some things for Murphy, a bed and some proper dog food. I only left him for about half an hour. He was fast asleep when I left so I thought he'd be OK. All the windows were open for air . . . But he must have woken up and got upset and then just chewed everything.'

'You didn't do anything wrong,' I say, leaning over the seat and giving her a hug. 'Dogs stay in cars all the time. He's just a nutcase.'

'Mad, bad, and dangerous to know. I am so sorry I got you into this . . . ' Jack says apologetically.

'I couldn't go to work,' Mum says miserably. 'I tried to leave him in the house but he went berserk and clawed at the door. Then I tried to get him settled in the garage. I bought him some lovely toys to play with . . . ' Her voice breaks and I watch her shoulders hunch. 'But he howled like a demon and jumped up at the windows. I thought he was going to crash through because they're not double glazed.'

'We'll have to take him back to the animal shelter. Let's do it now. I'll take him in and explain everything,' Jack says.

'Oh no . . . ' Mum says. 'Jade's dad wouldn't like that . . . We'll have to wait until he comes home and see what he says.'

'Oh, Mum—don't be ridiculous. We can't keep a dog that can't be left alone and eats the insides of cars. It's bonkers.'

Mum sniffs miserably. 'I'm not doing anything until your dad is home. He's the boss, you know that, Jade.'

I could make the joke that he always says that about her, but I think she's beyond cheering up. 'Your middle name must be trouble,' I tell Murphy crossly. He whines and looks at me with pathetic eyes.

Jack wraps his arms around me and I snuggle into him. Misery overwhelms me. This is not an appropriate time to tell Mum about troubles one and two—or to think about Murphy's fate when we take him back to the dogs' home.

Jack has gone home by the time Dad gets back. Jack's still offering to take Murphy back to the animal shelter—which I think is really brave and sweet of him. Mum has cooked Murphy a gorgeous supper. It's really sad—like the last meal of a condemned man.

Dad shrugs off his jacket and flops down in a chair. 'I never thought I'd get sick of London. But I was that pleased to leave the smoke this time,' he says quietly and I sense a terrible weariness in him.

Falteringly Mum tells Dad about Murphy.

'Not your fault, sweetheart,' he says reassuringly, leaning across and giving her a kiss. 'He'll take a bit of settling down. I'm going to be at home for a bit—I'll get him sorted.'

Mum gives a sharp cry of despair. 'What happened?'

'They gave me the elbow. The old one-two-heave-ho walk the bleeding plank.'

'But it's your company,' I say angrily. 'How can they do that? You started Stevens and Co. It's even got our name!'

'I'm not a major shareholder any more and the board of directors don't want me. They voted me out. I don't have the right image, apparently. They want a berk in a suit—some flash geezer to chat up the customers. Don't matter. Don't worry about it, Princess. I'll start again,' Dad adds with an attempt at cheerfulness. He looks down at Murphy, who is lying at his feet, and tries to smile as he says, 'Saved your bacon, anyway, my old son.'

We have our meal. I try to think of something cheerful to tell them about school. I will find the right time to tell them about my bad conduct ticket, but not now.

After supper Dad says he'll take Murphy out for a walk

round the park. It's more like a bout of all-in wrestling because Murphy hasn't a clue about walking on a lead and hates having his collar on. Dad pulls on his waterproof coat. 'I always knew I should have been a lion tamer,' he jokes, as he sets off into the dark, damp night.

Mum sighs and I just know she is thinking of an Andrex-type puppy and the fun we could have had with it. Guilt and misery are filling me up. I decide to do something positive—so I reluctantly get out my art portfolio. I stay in the kitchen with Mum because I think she needs cheering up.

In the art lesson Mr Garforth suggested I draw an illustrated family tree. Teachers like it when you take up their suggestions—they always think their ideas are the best. So I start by writing my name at the top of a sheet of paper.

'Why did you call me Jade?' I ask Mum.

'We wanted to name you after something precious and I thought Jade was pretty. Your dad liked Ruby and Pearl, but I thought they were too old-fashioned.'

'Wow!' I mutter thankfully. 'What a lucky escape. Ruby! What a moniker!'

'You sound just like your dad when you say that,' Mum says, and she smiles.

I draw little lines and put Mum's and Dad's names in. Then I draw more little lines and put Nana and Grandad in and the dates of everyone's birthdays.

'What was Grandad's full name?' I ask Mum.

'Edward Taylor Grant. What are you doing, Jadey?' she asks, looking over my shoulder. I can't see her face but I feel her tense.

'Family tree,' I say, writing Grandad's name in. 'Do you remember the names of your grandparents? Do you think Nana might have any old photos?'

'Maybe, I'll ask her when I phone,' Mum says miserably. 'But you won't be able to fill in anything on Dad's side.'

'I'll just put the names in. I don't have to do pictures of everyone.'

'He won't tell you the names,' Mum says. 'Don't mention it to him, Jade,' she adds and her voice is quite sharp.

I sit and doodle on a bit of scrap paper. 'Oh well, I may as well give this up then,' I say. 'If no one will tell me anything.'

'He doesn't know very much and what he does know he won't tell anyone. He only ever talked to me about it once . . . ' Mum shivers suddenly although the kitchen is warm. 'He had a terrible childhood, Jade. His mother . . . his mother . . . ' Mum swallows. 'She was a . . . ' Mum doesn't manage to get the word out.

I just sit and watch her and it's awful—like watching someone choking on a hot potato and not being able to help them.

'His mother was a drug addict,' Mum finally mutters.

'Oh that's sad, another victim of the swinging sixties, I suppose,' I say, trying to sound cool about it.

'She was a heroin addict. She'd do anything for money. There were three boys and they all had different fathers.' Mum is talking quickly now. 'I could have forgiven her all of that but she neglected them. She used to put all the dirty washing in a cupboard and forget about it. There was never enough to eat. The boys were in and out of care. Once, your dad was taken away to a home and they gave him vitamin injections. He grew six inches in six months.'

Mum's eyes are full of tears. I don't really want to hear any more but it's as if she can't stop now. 'After the homes and the failed foster families it was approved school. Of course he was in trouble. He'd never had a family or anyone to care about him. He doesn't want you to know anything about it. He just wants to pretend that his life started when we met. All he ever wanted was a family to call his own.'

Suddenly I see life spread out like a patchwork before me. I have seen the individual pieces but never the whole pattern before. So many things suddenly make sense: Dad's hatred of waste, his unexpected generosity, and his love for Nana despite her nagging—all explained. Poor Dad.

'Well, he's got a family and a home now. He's even got Nana. Don't cry, Mum, please. He's had a fantastic life since he met you. He always says you were the best thing that ever happened to him, and it's true.' I hope I have found the right thing to say. I hate to see her sobbing.

'Oh, Jadey.' Mum lifts her head from her hands and looks at me. There is bleak misery in her eyes. 'You don't know the half of it.'

The back door bangs. 'We're home,' Dad calls out. We can hear him in the utility room talking to Murphy. 'Givvus them plates of meat, you old ugly mug. Don't know how you get so lathered in mud just walking around the park. He was ever so good,' he calls to us. 'He's getting the idea of walking on the lead. We'll have him at Crufts yet, you see.' He laughs. 'Best delinquent category.'

Mum has jumped up like a frightened deer and she wipes her face quickly with the tea towel. 'I'll put the kettle on,' she says thickly. Then she adds with a little sigh. 'He does love that dog so.'

'Oh gawd . . . ' I say with a groan. What have I done? My life seems to be turning into a nightmare. I escape up to my bedroom and rip the work in my art folder into little tiny bits and put them in the bin. My hands falter when I come to the sketch of Finn, I look at the harsh black lines and remember his kindness to me at the cinema. Guilt washes over me. I rip the paper to the size of confetti, until it is so small I can't tear it any more. I wish life was like a video and you could rewind it and replay it with different things happening. There are so many things I would like to do differently.

I look down at my empty portfolio and try not to panic. I try telling myself that it is quite simple—I will have to think of a new topic or drop art. But the reality is that I am terrified of heaping more worry on Mum and Dad. I've always been their perfect princess—I don't know if I can cope with the new role of rebel. Anyway, I've got them lumbered with Murphy—one delinquent in the family is enough.

Jack is working—there's no comfort to be had there—so I sit with my headphones on and play music really loudly. 'You'll be deaf before you're twenty,' Nana would say.

I don't care. I want to anaesthetize my brain.

# 7

There never seems to be the right moment to tell Mum and Dad about the letter coming from school. Life is pretty difficult at home. Dad is pretending to be cheerful, but he whistles a bit too hard and tells too many jokes. He is organizing his finances and the Range Rover is to be repaired and sold.

Mum is in a sweat. Literally. She starts to clean the house. Honestly, you'd think we live in a slum or something. She buys all this special foaming stuff to clean the drains and little brushes to poke down the overflows of the sinks. You'd think she was fighting an imminent outbreak of Bubonic Plague.

Poor old Murph gets bathed and covered in special potions to stop him getting ticks and fleas. 'Where's he going to get ticks from?' I ask. 'He only ever gets to walk around the park.'

'He'll soon be able to go off the lead and out somewhere exciting, when he learns to come when he's called,' Mum says grimly.

All this house cleaning makes me wonder if we are going to be moving. I am starting to get a bit fed up because my parents don't talk to me about things. There's a lot of whispering which stops when I come into the room. Something is up.

I will be sorry if we have to leave this house, not so much for myself but for Dad. This house is like his baby. He conceived and built it and he is just so proud of it. I hope for his sake we can stay here.

What with all the cleaning chaos and stuff being turned out from wardrobes, there is never a quiet calm moment to tell them about my problem at school. I get this stupid idea in my head that the letter won't arrive. I make myself believe that Big Willie (dear, kind Mrs Williams) will have had second thoughts. After all, Jack and I have been model pupils for so long, she is bound to reconsider and decide not to burden our parents with news of our very first trip down delinquency lane.

Fat bloody chance. The miserable old fart-face posts the letter first class and it arrives with an ominous thud on the doormat on Saturday morning. I bet, as she licked the envelope, she thought to herself, This will make sure they have a good weekend. Vicious or what?

Dad gets to the letters before I do. (Shame!) I follow him into the kitchen. He rather absentmindedly puts them behind the fruit bowl.

'Anything important?' Mum asks anxiously. She has a permanently worried frown on her face at the moment.

'Only bills and junk mail,' I sing out gaily. 'Are you ready to go, Dad? I don't want to be late.' I know I'm only delaying trouble, but I still do it.

The door to *Flower Power* is open and Nola comes out to meet us. 'Hi, Jade. Hello, Rick. How are things?' she says.

Dad does the thumbs down sign to her. 'Oh, you poor thing.' She takes hold of his arm. 'Come on upstairs and I'll make you a coffee. You can tell me all about it. The workshop's a pigsty, sorry, Jade,' she calls to me.

She's not kidding. I don't think it's been tidied all week. I sigh and reach for a bin bag. Above my head I can hear the rise and fall of voices and I feel unreasonably irritated that I have been left down here working while Nola and Dad are drinking coffee. Anyway, why does Nola think that Dad wants to talk to her about his troubles?

An hour passes and Dad is still upstairs talking to Nola. I remember all the things that have to be done to open up the shop and at nine o'clock I unlock the door and serve a customer. It's an old lady in a tatty tweed coat and woolly hat who wants to order some funeral flowers. I sit her down on a chair and get the black book out from under the counter. Her hands shake a bit as she takes the book and she starts to tell me all about her husband who has died. She goes on and on for ages. It's just as well no one else comes into the shop because I am kind of glued to the spot. It's awful. I could bawl like a baby. I don't really know what to say. 'Sorry' doesn't sound right. So I just nod and try to make sympathetic noises and listen as if it's the most important stuff I've ever been told in my life.

Finally I talk her through all the different arrangements, the flowers that are used, and how much they cost, because she hasn't got her reading glasses with her. 'I'm all at sixes and sevens,' she says.

It's really depressing. If it was me I would just choose the first one in the book and bolt. But she seems quite happy to look at everything. And after much deliberation and asking my advice she decides what she wants.

'I'm new, maybe I better get the owner. It's going to take me a bit of time to do this bit . . . ' I explain, as I get the order pad out. There're lots of details that I have to get right: times, places, names of people . . . names of undertakers. It's awful and I'm terrified I'll get something wrong.

'Oh no, dear, don't do that. Take as long as you like. It's been so nice to have you to talk to,' she says. 'I don't mind sitting here while you sort it out. It makes a change from sitting on my own.'

It's when she gets out this old leather-covered cheque book and starts writing out the cheque in spidery handwriting that I feel my eyes prickle with tears. If it was my shop I'd probably be giving her the wreath for nothing.

As she leaves she reaches out with her old woman's freckly hand and pats my arm. 'Thank you, dear, for all your help and patience. You're a very kind young lady.' And I feel really humble because I haven't done anything but listen.

I hear Nola and Dad coming down the stairs, still yakking, and I blow my nose and wipe my eyes quickly.

'I served a customer—flowers for a funeral—I hope I did it right. I jotted down her name and phone number just in case you need to check anything.' I hold out the order book to Nola.

She scans it and says, 'Perfect, Jade, well done.'

'You look a bit weepy,' Dad says, frowning at me anxiously.

'I think I've got a cold starting,' I lie.

'Finn's just come down from the attic for his breakfast, pop up and have a coffee with him,' Nola says kindly. It seems churlish to refuse though I dread seeing Finn and I walk up the stairs with reluctant footsteps.

I knock on the kitchen door because it seems kind of rude just to walk in on him. He opens the door swiftly. 'You don't have to knock—this isn't school,' he says abruptly.

'How are you?' I say with an attempt at cheerfulness. I move over to the window and look out, because it's easier than facing him. Dad is just getting into Mum's car. I wave but he doesn't see me.

'Would you like coffee and some toast?' Finn asks. I suddenly realize I am hungry and the smell of the hot bread is making my mouth water.

'Yes, please,' I say.

We sit opposite each other at the table. I spread marg thinly on my toast, inspecting it with all the concentration of a jeweller looking at a priceless diamond.

'I'm sorry to hear about your dad's business,' he mutters.

'Yeah, it's bad for him.'

'Will you have to move?'

I shrug in reply. Conversation stops while we eat. We avoid looking at each other. I wipe my mouth with my hanky—worried I have grease on my chin.

'I did some copies of the photos for you,' he says suddenly. He goes to the sink, rinses his hands and takes a brown envelope from the sideboard drawer. 'I wasn't sure which ones you wanted so I did a selection. I found one of your parents' wedding day.'

'Really? Can I see it?'

The photo shows a winter's day. Mum and Dad are standing under a bare tree and the ground is littered with dead leaves. Behind them is a grey stone building. I suppose it's a Register Office. They've never talked about their wedding and this is the first photo I've ever seen. I stare at it curiously. Mum is wearing a hideous pink suit that makes her look fat and Dad has a moustache and is wearing ghastly trousers. Despite their awful clothes they look young and happy. Nola is in the picture with them, no one else.

'Is this the only photo of their wedding?' I ask.

Finn nods.

The next picture I look at shows Mum when she is heavily pregnant. She's standing outside the shop next to a display of daffodils and Finn is holding her hand. He was a really cute little boy but I don't take too much notice of him. I am too busy staring at Mum's swollen belly that was me in hiding.

I blink back sudden hot tears. I'm not adopted—that is for sure. I hadn't thought I was upset by the idea until now. I'd thought I was all mature and sensible and could cope with it. But relief that I really do belong to Mum and Dad floods through me.

'I think that photo was taken a couple of weeks before you were born. Evidently I was a real pain and used to want to sit on your mam's lap so I could feel you kicking.' Finn laughs and I manage a weak smile.

'Thanks very much for the photos,' I whisper. I put

them all back in the envelope and hug it to me. He can have no idea how precious they are to me.

'I thought they'd be a help with your project,' he says. 'How's it going?'

'It's not. I've ripped everything up. I'm dropping art.'

Finn frowns at me. I add quickly, 'But thanks, anyway, for the photos. I'm really thrilled with them.'

'You should never tear up your work. Even if you're not pleased with it. It's a waste.'

'Everything I'd done was awful. I'm rubbish at art.'

'Oh, I don't know. You're good at cartoons,' he says a bit grimly.

'Yeah, well, I ripped all those up as well,' I say, pleased to set the record straight. I would like to say sorry but the words won't come out.

'Your mam and dad will be upset,' he says. 'Dropping out of school is one thing that really spooks parents. Believe me—I know. I bummed around for two years until I went back to college and Nola was on my back the whole time.'

I sigh and finish my coffee. 'I know, but I'm not getting anywhere with it. It was the wrong topic for me.'

Finn's eyes light up with sudden enthusiasm. His face breaks into this great big grin as he says, 'Hey! I've got it! Why don't you take photos from a baby's perspective and then turn them into cartoons?'

I gaze at him a bit blankly. 'You what?'

'Look, come down here and I'll show you what I mean.' He takes my arm and pulls me down onto the floor. I don't get down far enough and he tugs at me. I feel a real fool lying on the worn lino with him.

The worst thing is I have to make a real effort to stop myself staring into his face. Close-up he has beautiful skin, flawless and pale, and the longest eyelashes I've ever seen. (Life is so unfair—if I had lashes like that I would never have to wear mascara.)

He's explaining to me: 'You have to get right down,

infant-sized, and then look up at everything as if you are a baby. It's a different world. All you see are giant tables and people with legs like tree trunks.'

He stands up and grabs a spoon from the table. Then, kneeling on the floor, he leans over me. 'Then, imagine it, you get placed in a high chair and your mother waves a huge spoon in front of your face, it's laden with food you don't want to eat and the spoon is nearly as big as your mouth. You're terrified. Then she takes you out in your buggy and all you see is rushing clouds and the tops of trees.'

'Yes!' I whisper excitedly, looking up into his face, just as if I'm a baby and he's my mum. 'And then some gross person comes and pokes their ugly mug right under your rain hood and talks gibberish to you. It must be a nightmare being a baby—no wonder they scream all the time.'

'Thanks for the compliment,' he says grinning. Then he gets up and holds his hand out to me. I take his hand and he slowly pulls me to my feet.

'It's a brilliant idea, thanks,' I say, pulling my hair back into a ponytail, suddenly embarrassed by our closeness.

'That's OK,' he mutters.

'I better go down and do some work,' I say.

'Yeah.'

Then he says suddenly, 'I could take you out to Farringdon Forest tomorrow. We could take some photos under the trees and I'll develop the prints, if you like. I'd take you in the van, not on my bike,' he adds quickly. He turns away, avoiding my eyes. 'Only if you want to,' he adds.

'Thanks, yes.' I am unable to say anything else I am so surprised.

I walk downstairs in a daze. I have the feeling I have just been asked out, but I'm not really sure. For a moment I am angry with myself because I am so confused. Then I feel guilty about Jack and that makes me even more annoyed. I'm being such a fool! There is nothing to feel guilty about—is there? We are going to take some photos—and that is all. I tell myself to get a grip but it is weird to feel like this about Finn—all kind of churned up and excited. It's worse than weird—it's crazy. I have to stop it now. I calm myself down by telling myself that Finn is just being kind to me because he liked me when he was a little kid.

Still, he has been good to me. So that's OK. I can allow myself a feeling of warmth towards him. When I think about it he's been more than good to me. He saved me at the cinema and now he's sorted out my life. It's gratitude that I feel. (Sigh of relief.) Gratitude is OK. I can cope with that. It's the other feelings that freak me out. The urge I have to touch him, to move closer to him and to make him smile.

To chase away these thoughts I think about how much I'd like to paint him. Reminding myself that my interest in him is purely artistic—not romantic. All I really want is to see if I can get the milky colour of his skin just right, and capture the way his freckles look as if they've been dabbed on with a dusty finger.

Nola goes out on her deliveries and the shop is very quiet. I get out my sketchpad and start to pencil in Finn's face. It's strange how easily it comes to me. I pencil in his distinctive eyebrows and the long sharp angle of his jaw. I stare down at my work, and suddenly I am frightened. I tear the page out, screw it up, and throw it in the bin.

Then I start a new sketch—and this time I draw Jack. I know Jack's face so well I can outline it without even having to think. I am on automatic pilot. He is so beautiful all the proportions of his face are exactly as they should be.

'Still drawing pictures of lover boy?' Finn's voice makes me jump.

'Whatever are you doing, creeping about like that? You startled me,' I snap.

'I wasn't creeping. You were miles away.' He looks over my shoulder and I pull my sketchbook away quickly. 'He's too good looking,' Finn says dismissively. 'His mother should have dropped him on his nose. He'd be much better for it.'

'That's a really tight thing to say,' I say, stung by his tone. 'Jack's had a really awful time with his mother. She's done worse things to him than drop him on his nose, I can tell you.'

Finn shrugs. 'There's no need for him to take it out on other people.'

'He doesn't!' I say hotly.

'What was he doing at the cinema? Making an arse of himself with that little slapper? Why is he messing around with her when he's got a girl like you?' He stops and a guarded look comes over his face. He scowls at me darkly. It's like being faced by a thunderstorm. I turn away.

'You don't understand,' I say a bit wearily. If I'm honest I know he's got a point. But thinking about Sybil and the way she plays Jack along makes me feel tired. I don't want to think about it. I've forgiven Jack—things are fine between us. That's all that matters.

'No—I don't suppose I do understand,' he says coolly.

He walks towards the door; if I don't speak quickly I will be too late. 'Finn . . . ' I say. He stops but doesn't turn. For a moment my courage fails. Then I say quickly, 'I would like to go out tomorrow and take some photos, if it's still OK. I've only got a week to get the whole project finished and it's meant to be half a term's work.'

'OK, pick you up about eleven. Wear something warm,' he adds (as if I'm a moron and might turn up in a mini skirt and high heels!).

'Finn,' my voice is hardly audible, but all the same he stops in the doorway and turns. 'Thanks, for thinking about my project . . . and for the photos . . . '

'It's OK,' he mutters. But he gives me a quick smile. I've never met anyone who smiles as he does—it's like when the sun comes out on a dull winter's day. Pure magic!

He leaves and I begin to scrabble around in the wastepaper bin. I find the sketch I started. I look down carefully at the image of Finn and smooth the creases with my fingers. Finn's right—it's a waste to throw your work away. I carefully put the crushed piece of paper into the back of my sketchpad and stow it away in my bag. I can make a copy on a fresh piece of paper and finish it. It's loads better than the stuff I normally do. I must have been bonkers to throw it away.

# 8

The parents are in a major stress over the letter. Honestly—you'd think it was the end of the world to get one bad conduct ticket.

'For heaven's sake!' I snap. 'Some people collect enough to paper their bedroom.'

'You're not some people,' Dad says. 'You are our precious little girl. I'm going to have a word with that bloody Jack . . .'

'Oh no you're not!' I yell. 'You're being absolutely stupid. I've told you! We weren't doing anything. We were talking. You all have filthy, sex-obsessed minds. And that old bitch Froggit is the worst of the lot. She's just a frustrated old spinster who thinks the whole world is doing whatever it is she would like to be up to. And we weren't!' Having yelled that at them at top volume I flounce upstairs and lock myself in my bedroom.

First Dad comes and knocks on the door. He sounds really upset. 'Sweetheart, Princess,' he says. 'I'm sorry, darlin'. I believe you. Please come out and have some dinner. Your mum and I know you're a good girl . . .'

'Go away and leave me alone,' I snap.

Later Mum comes and rattles the door handle. 'Jade, please open the door. I've got some supper here for you. You must be hungry after a day at work. Daddy and I are sorry if we've upset you. Please have something to eat.'

Mum sounds just about ready to cry. (You'd think I was going to die from malnutrition from missing one meal.) I sigh and get up off the bed. You'd have to have a heart of stone not to answer the door to Mum when she's snivelling.

'You know I'm spoilt to death,' I say really coldly, as she comes in and puts a tray down next to the television. She's made a little salad with all my favourite things in it and a tiny fresh pizza dotted with pieces of pepperoni.

'I met Sybil when I was shopping and I said she should come for supper sometime soon,' Mum says meekly. I take a mouthful of pizza and don't answer.

'She seems such a lonely girl,' Mum says. 'I felt sorry for her.'

'Lonely!' I snort. 'You've got to be joking. She's been out with just about every boy in the school. They queue up to date her. You want to talk to Sybil about inappropriate behaviour, not me,' I add bitterly.

'Oh dear,' Mum says a bit absentmindedly. 'What a worry for her parents. I hope she's being sensible. Though I suppose with her mum being a doctor . . . ' Mum's voice trails off. 'Jade,' Mum takes a deep breath and says, 'I really think I ought to have a little talk with you.'

An alarm bell rings in my head. I just know for a certainty that whatever it is she is going to say I don't want to hear. I pick at the salad with my fingers and ignore her.

'But . . . I don't know,' Mum says with sigh. 'I hope I'm not being a coward. But I thought it might be better to get you a book.'

From her apron pocket Mum produces a pink-striped bag and holds it out to me. I carry on eating, investigating my salad as if a slug might be hiding among the lettuce. From the tail of my eye I see her undo the bag and hold out a lurid purple and silver paperback book. I can see that it's got some awful naff title about girls and sex. It's the kind of thing the year nines pass around and snigger over.

'For heaven's sake!' I snap. 'What on earth are you thinking of! I don't need that. We've had so much sex education at school we're all sick to death of fallopian tubes and gestation. We've had so many talks and free condoms it's a miracle we aren't all taking an extra AS in gynaecology.'

'We're just worried about you . . .' Mum says.

'Why?'

'Dad says you and Finn Casey . . . were kissing . . .' Mum's face is scarlet. Anger makes me cruel. I give her a death stare and she gulps and continues, 'He's a lot older than you are. I don't worry about you and Jack . . . but Finn . . .'

'Oh, and why don't you worry about me and Jack?' (I had decided that I wouldn't speak to her—because she really hates it when I do that—but curiosity gets the better of me.)

'I've always thought he was more like . . . well, more like your brother than your boyfriend,' Mum blurts out.

'What?'

'I suppose it's having been friends for such a long time . . .' Mum adds lamely. 'He's a lovely boy, we are very fond of him, but he's not really like a boyfriend, is he?'

'Full marks for observation,' I scoff.

'No one told me anything about sex when I was your age,' Mum mutters, her voice so low and miserable I can hardly hear her. 'We did biology at school, but I didn't really know anything. I don't want it to be like that for you, Jade. I was so ignorant and stupid.'

For one awful moment I think she's going to launch into some confessional about her and Dad. I really can't cope.

'Thanks a lot,' I say swiftly.

'I don't know if the book will be any use, but you can always ask me anything.' After what she's just told me there doesn't seem much point. Talk about the blind leading the blind. (Thank you, Nana, for another naff saying!)

There is a long silence. Mum watches me eat. I refuse to look at her. I finish the pizza. She takes the tray away.

Alone in the silence of my room, I throw myself down on the bed and think about how unhappy I am. Opening the book I see that I have arrived at the chapter entitled, 'How to know if a boy fancies you'! It's like some awful omen. I know exactly how to tell if a boy doesn't fancy you. I throw the book across the room and bury myself under my duvet.

As if he knows I am thinking about him, Jack phones me. 'I've just finished a song. Can I come round?' he asks. He sounds all excited and happy. He gets a kind of high when he's written something good.

Speaking to him works on me like a magic spell. I get up and shower and get changed into some clean jeans. Downstairs Mum and Dad are in the kitchen, looking at account books and doing sums with a calculator. I check that we've got a tub of chocolate ice cream in the freezer and put some Coke to chill in the fridge.

'Jack's coming round,' I call out to them.

'You can make yourselves comfortable in the sitting room. We'll be busy with this for hours yet,' Mum says. It crosses my mind that this might be a ploy to keep Jack out of my bedroom. I sigh.

I stop in the middle of the kitchen and say, 'You won't say anything to Jack, will you? Only he's been really depressed lately and it really wouldn't do him any good to think you don't trust him.'

'Whatever you say, Princess. Your mum and I have absolute faith in you,' Dad says.

'Are we going to have to move?' I ask, looking down at the bank accounts and papers spread across the table. Mum and Dad exchange glances. 'It's only a house, after all, isn't it?' I say. And then, because I am so happy Jack is coming to see me, I smile at them and say, 'We don't really need all these spare bedrooms, do we?'

'No,' Dad says, a bit sadly. 'And your mum will make

wherever we live into a little palace, we know that. I do need to raise some capital, but don't you worry your head about it, Princess. I'll make sure you and your mum are OK.'

'I know you will,' I say, and I kiss his forehead as I pass.

Jack arrives with his guitar. He hasn't eaten so Mum makes him some sandwiches and then we pig out on chocolate banana splits. Finally he gets the guitar out of the case and sings his new song to me. It is wicked.

'You must send it off to a music publisher. It's amazing,' I say. 'Sing it for me again.'

The song is called 'I Sign your Name with a Kiss' and it's a really knock-out romantic song. It's wonderful watching Jack sing, he closes his eyes and leans his head to one side. His hair flops in a golden curtain, hiding his eyes, it's just about the most beautiful thing I've ever seen. I love him so much I want to cry.

Hearing the song for a second time gives me a chance to listen to the lyrics. It's about missing the person you love, about being parted and writing letters. I think about the notes Jack and I pass to each other in class and smile.

Then he sings the chorus:

> *'I sign your name with a kiss*
> *Because you're the one*
> *The one I really miss.*
> *I sign your name with a kiss*
> *And I count the hours—*
> *The long slow hours—*
> *Until the time is right*
> *For us to meet*
> *And I will see you again.'*

And then this terrible feeling worms its way into my head. It's like when water seeps from a fractured pipe. At first there's just a sinister droplet, then a slow gathering until wham—a flood hissing and spurting in my brain.

And then I know with absolute certainty that this song has not been written for me or about me.

For a while I am just frozen with shock. I sit with my mouth hanging open and my breath coming a bit too fast. I think I'm having some kind of panic attack because I can feel the blood drumming in my ears. Jack doesn't even notice. He sings the song through again. Singing it obviously makes him feel good. Then, without so much as a glance at me, he starts on some more of his love songs. There's nothing in them about a short dark girl who still looks about twelve, nothing about a bestest friend, or about a girl called Jade. In fact nothing about a girl at all . . .

Finally I say, 'I'm going to take Murphy into the garden for a bit.'

'OK.' Jack is all lazy and pleased with himself. 'I'll come too.' He tries to link his arm through mine but I pull away and pretend I am busy looking for my old trainers.

It's cold and dark in the garden. Murphy is off— galloping around the lawn like a giant rocking horse and peeing up against the bushes. I walk quickly right to the end of the garden, past the beech hedge that separates the flower garden from the veg patch, past the raspberry canes that Mum prizes so much. I think about how much my parents love this house—the plants and trees they have put in the garden and how they've cherished everything and I feel as if my heart will break from sadness.

'Jade.' Jack's voice is high and anxious. He has followed me. We are in the darkest shadows, near to the summerhouse that Mum never gets to sit in because she is too busy weeding and planting and picking sweetpeas. 'What's the matter?'

'We're probably going to have to move from here,' I say angrily. 'My dad needs to start a new business.'

'Oh, Jade, I'm so sorry,' he says. He sounds sorry, but he also sounds relieved. 'You're not angry with me, are you?' he says in a whisper.

'No, I'm not angry,' I mutter. Then strangely Finn

comes into my mind. I ask myself what Finn would do in a situation like this. I know the answer—it doesn't make me feel good—but it does give me the strength to say calmly, 'Jack, can we do a bit of straight talking?'

'What do you mean?'

At that moment Murphy comes crashing through the blackcurrant bushes to find me. He barges into me and licks my face as if we have been parted for hours instead of minutes. 'Get off, you big lollark,' I say, elbowing him away. He smells of Chappie and compost, not the nicest mixture in the world, and he's just wiped his greasy tongue around my ear. (It's just as well there's not going to be any passionate snogging out here in the garden for me.)

I turn back to Jack. I can just make out the pale oval of his face in the darkness. His eyes are shadowed like a skull. 'Tell me whose name you sign with a kiss?' I ask in a cheerful conversational kind of tone that disguises my real feelings.

'What do you mean?'

'As Miss Langford tells us, repetition is tedious. Don't keep asking me what I mean. Just tell me who you were thinking about when you wrote that song.'

'I was just thinking about being in love.' Jack sounds sulky.

'Jack—just tell me the truth—please.'

It's awful—Jack bursts into tears. I can hear the sobs, and his face is distorted as if I am seeing him under water, but I am powerless to move to comfort him. I am frozen within my own hurt, caught like a poor perished creature inside a slow-moving glacier of pain.

Eventually he wipes his eyes on his sleeve and says, 'I've always thought we would get married and end up like your mum and dad. It's all I've ever wanted. I swear it, Jade. You are the only real family I've ever had. I adore you. I could never imagine loving anyone as much as I love you . . . ' his voice trails away miserably.

'OK. And then what happened?' I prompt gently. I know I am not going to like what I hear—but I want to hear it anyway. I am tired of being in the dark. I want to know the truth. 'Tell me, Jack,' I say firmly.

'This summer something happened—this summer I met Xavier . . . '

'Xavier?' I echo. Xavier is the French boy Jack has been writing to. I swallow hard and try not to cry out—but I think I must have made some kind of sound because Jack starts crying again.

This time he sounds so desperate I move across and take him in my arms. I feel like a survivor in a disaster clinging for comfort to some other injured soul and praying for rescue.

'It's not the end of the world . . . ' I say, trying not to cry.

'I don't want to be gay . . . ' he says. 'I'm scared, Jade. I'm so scared.'

'What are you scared of?'

'I'm scared of how I feel and I'm scared because I don't know if he feels the same way or if I imagined it all. When we're together it isn't like anything else that has ever happened to me. It's as if we're the only two people in the whole world. As if I've just met the other half of me— and without him I'm incomplete. I just keep wishing he was a girl . . . '

'Don't say that—it's crazy,' I say, pulling his head down and trying to wipe the wetness from his face with my fingers. 'You wouldn't love him if he was a girl. You love him for what he is. What's so terrible about being gay? Apart from all the stupid jokes people make at school.'

He pulls away from me quite angrily. 'Oh—it's OK for you, isn't it? You're lucky little Jade, the perfect princess. You don't know how scary it feels to be different. I want to be normal. I want to be like everyone else. I don't want to end up as some sad gay boy hanging around bars.'

His anger makes me recoil from him. 'Jack! For heaven's sake,' I beg. 'You drop this on me and then suddenly you act as if it's all my fault.'

Jack moves into the summerhouse and sits down. He buries his head in his hands. 'I'm sorry, Jade,' he mutters.

'Look, let's just argue about one thing at a time, shall we?' I say gently. 'You can have a go at me another night about my fabulous luck.' I take his arm and lean into his shoulder. 'Just remember no one can make you anything you're not. You don't have to live to anyone else's stereotype. No one will make you promiscuous if you don't want to be. There must be lots of gay men who never go near a bar or pick people up. Think about it—there are plenty of women who behave like that, but I don't assume I'll do it just because I'm female.'

He wraps his arms around me and I hear him sigh. 'All through the summer I kept on planning how I was going to ask you to go steady. See if I could buy you an engagement ring, and then I met—'

I break in quickly because I can't really bear to hear him say that name again. It just makes me want to crack up. I swallow my hurt. 'Jack,' I say gently. 'That's really sweet, but we both know it would never have worked. We are too close—aren't we?'

'I just wanted it to happen so much,' he says. 'And then I thought getting off with Sybil might do the trick. She's so experienced. I thought she might cure me.'

'Sybil!' I stutter. 'Crikey, Jack! In the fourteen years I've known you I've never thought of you as stupid—but I think I could be about to revise my opinion. You'd be more likely to catch something than get a cure from Sybil.'

'Can you forgive me for being so stupid? I know I've hurt you.'

'Yes, of course I forgive you,' I whisper. Hurt doesn't seem much of a word to describe how I am feeling. Still, I suppose there's not a lot of poetry in being lied to and let down.

'We'll always be bestest friends, won't we?' he whispers, holding on to me tightly.

'Yes,' I whisper back.

Murphy comes into the summerhouse and nuzzles at me. I have Jack on one side of me and Murphy on the other. I have to take what comfort I can from the warmth and nearness of them, and the knowledge that they both love me, in their own way. But what I really need is sticky plaster around my poor aching heart. 'Come on, let's go in. I'm cold,' I say at last. And we walk back to the house hand in hand, looking for all the world like star-struck lovers. Well—appearances can be deceptive, can't they?

# 9

After Jack has left I feel really depressed. It's like when Grandad died. Not only have I lost Jack but also some special time of my life has ended. It's a really melancholy feeling knowing that something precious has vanished and will never come back. All the plans I'd made in my head about Jack and me have disappeared, killed stone dead by his announcement. I feel sore and bruised and a bit sick. I am unable to eat or do anything but sit in front of the TV like a zombie.

As if all that wasn't bad enough my parents get themselves into another right old stress because we are meant to be visiting Nana tomorrow and I say I won't go.

'But we always go over to see her on the first weekend of half term,' Mum says. 'Nana looks forward to it. She'll be so disappointed not to see you.'

'I've got work to do. I've got to do loads of photos and sketches before school starts again. We've only just got back from visiting her.' I know I sound like a sulky little kid but I can't help it. Can't they see I am in pain? Why don't they go away and leave me alone?

'It won't be the same spending a day at the seaside without our little princess,' Dad says longingly.

'Oh, for heaven's sake, you must have had a life before I arrived on the scene!' I snap. 'Can't you just enjoy going out together and let me do my own thing?'

I see the hurt in their faces and I feel awful. But they have boxed me into a corner. I've lied and told them I am spending the day with Jack. I'm not comfortable with this fib—it has grown and spread into multiple untruths until I am totally irritable. Telling lies is like having a big gobby lump of chewing gum stuck on the sole of your trainer—it drives you crazy. I vow I won't do it again. Next time they can have the truth—even if they don't like it.

'Anyway you can't take Murphy into Nana's house. So it's best that I stay and look after him,' I mutter.

'You won't let him off his lead, will you, Jade?' Dad says anxiously. 'He's a real pain about coming when he's called and he might run away. Jack will help you with him, won't he?'

'Oh yes,' I say, wondering if Finn likes dogs.

I'm actually quite nervous about going out with Finn. I get quite upset and angry when I can't decide what to wear. (I don't want him to think I've gone to too much trouble and got dressed up for him!) I keep thinking about the years that I've spent hanging around with Jack. How I've never had a proper date. Never kissed a boy—except for Jack. It makes me feel terrible.

Mum and Dad leave quite early and I am so desperate I start reading the book Mum gave me. But it makes me feel bad—really bad. There's a whole chapter called 'Don't Worry About Kissing'. It goes on and on about how girls worry all the time about the right way to kiss a boy. It even says that some girls practise on their hands—which seems to me seriously weird. I can honestly say that until I read that chapter I hadn't had any particular worry about kissing—but after reading it I'm petrified. I am convinced that there must be some special way to kiss that Sybil knows about and I don't.

Because I spend so much time reading and throwing clothes around I'm not ready when the *Flower Power* van arrives. Finn comes round to the back door and that confuses me because I have rushed to open the front door. I run back to the kitchen and unlock the back door.

'Why did you come round here?' I ask.

'I don't know,' he says with a shrug. 'I'm a back door kind of person.'

'I'm nearly ready. I won't be a minute. Come in—do you want a coffee?'

He's looking a bit sulky. 'No, we ought to get going. The light goes early on these short days,' he says gruffly.

Heaven knows why I've been worrying about him kissing me! He hardly looks in my direction and doesn't seem the least bit pleased to see me. I wonder if he's regretting offering to do these photos.

'Do you mind if we take Murphy with us? He's our delinquent dog.'

'I know,' Finn says shortly. I suppose Dad has been telling Nola about Murphy.

'He's my early Christmas present,' I say with an attempt at cheerfulness.

I grab a blanket and a couple of dog towels from the utility room. 'He loves mud. I hope he won't make the van too dirty. Unfortunately he can't be left alone. He's suffering from battered-dog-syndrome.'

Murphy is not keen on getting into the van. In the end I have to use a piece of cold chicken from the fridge as bait and lure him in.

'Have you made sure the doors of the house are locked? And you'll need a warm coat and some gloves,' Finn says a bit curtly. 'It's always blowing a gale at Farringdon.'

I hate the way he talks to me as if I'm a kid (although I had forgotten to lock the front door). I sigh a bit as I get my ski jacket and gloves. I suppose this is what you have to expect from someone who bathed you when you were a baby. To him I will always be a child.

He doesn't talk when he's driving. I quite like that. I hate people who yak away and don't appear to be taking any notice of pedestrians and other vehicles.

Murphy sits with his head on my shoulder and licks my cheek at intervals. When we stop at the traffic lights

Finn smiles at me. 'That dog's very devoted to you, isn't he?' he says.

It's lovely when Finn smiles. It makes me feel just a tiny bit happy—something along the size of the evening star when it appears in the night sky. Just a twinkle of light in the blackness of my mood, but better than nothing.

'I'm really only a substitute. Dad's the real love of Murphy's life.'

The city is overcast and grey but when we get out into the countryside the sky turns a wonderful blue and the sun comes out. We park the van in the car park at Farringdon Forest. It's a huge great expanse of wood and moor with a radio mast at the top of a pine-covered hillside. It looks dark and mysterious and a bit frightening. The air is icy, much colder than in the city, and the wind whips at my face when I get out of the van and catches in my throat. The last time I tasted air like this—tingly and clean as ice cream—was when we were skiing in Austria.

'It's lovely here,' I say to Finn, managing a smile.

We set off along a bridle path and because it's early in the day for dog walkers we have the place to ourselves. It's just as well because Murphy goes crazy. I suppose he can smell all the rabbits and things in the woods and he is desperate to be running around among the trees. He tugs and chokes and it takes both of us to hang on to his lead. Yellow foam and saliva gather around his muzzle and when he breathes in it sounds like gravel being quarried. But still he won't give in and stop pulling.

Breathlessly Finn says to me, 'He's going to kill himself at this rate. He'll have heart failure in a minute. Can't we let him have a run around? He's sure to come back when he's tired.'

I am too worried about Murphy to put up much resistance. Also my arms feel as if they have been pulled from their sockets. 'Are you sure there aren't any sheep around here?' I question. 'I don't want him getting shot by a farmer.'

Finn shakes his head. 'It's just woods for miles, he'll be OK.'

We release the choke chain and Murphy is off as if he's been fired from a cannon. 'He came from the dog's home—he's a reject,' I say sadly.

'Your dad must be a saint to put up with him,' Finn grumbles, rubbing his chafed hands. 'He's a monster and he's as strong as an ox.'

'Yes, he is a pain, he doesn't do anything right,' I admit. 'Jack keeps on offering to take him back to the dogs' home. But Dad won't hear of it. To be honest I think Dad loves Murphy all the more because he's such hard work. I suppose it's a challenge.'

'He's a good bloke, your dad,' Finn says.

Now we are free of Murphy Finn starts explaining about taking photos. I am used to just pointing my camera and pressing the button, but he explains all kinds of things that I'd never thought of. I find it really difficult to concentrate. Partly because I'm still upset about Jack, but also because I keep watching out for Murphy, who is a ginger shadow racing through the trees, barking like a canine lunatic.

Eventually Finn gives a crooked kind of smile and says, 'Do you want to just shoot a couple of films and see what we get?'

'Yes, will you keep an eye on Murphy?'

'What difference is watching him going to make?' Finn asks.

'I'm just worried he'll get lost and Dad will never forgive me.'

Finn puts his fingers in his mouth and emits an ear-shattering whistle. Murphy emerges from the forest and wades through the irrigation ditch at the side of the path. Then he throws himself on Finn, putting his paws up on Finn's chest and licking his face. Finn doesn't seem to mind. He rubs Murphy's ears and calls him a good dog.

'See—he comes back—there's no problem,' Finn says,

pushing Murphy down. 'Apart from the fact that he's soaking wet and smells like a sewer.'

We wander off down a side path and, miracle of miracles, Murphy walks next to us just like a proper grown-up-fully-brain-functioning dog. I take some pictures from underneath the trees as if I am a baby in a pram and some gorgeous shots of the sky. Finn's camera is lovely and I'm really enjoying pretending to be a photographer. I take a picture of Finn and Murphy together and wish I'd told Mum and Dad the truth about who I was coming out with, because I realize I won't be able to show it to them even though I think it's the best shot I've taken.

The first hint of trouble starts when we meet a man with two Border collies; he is training these two dogs with a whistle and the sound of it sends Murphy insane. He races around with the collies, barking and snapping at their heels. It's obvious he just wants to play but the man gets really cross.

'Can't you keep your dog under control? He's upsetting my training programme!' he snaps at Finn.

'He's out for a run. He's just doing what dogs do,' Finn retorts. At that moment the collies get fed up with being chased and turn on Murphy. There's an outburst of furious yapping and snapping and for a couple of seconds you can't see the dogs—there's just a Catherine wheel of ginger and black and white fur rolling on the ground.

The man whistles until I think he's going to have a seizure and his dogs reluctantly leave Murphy and come to heel. It's sickeningly impressive. Finn whistles for Murphy. I *will* Murphy to come back to us and show the man he can behave, but no such luck—Murphy runs off like a kangaroo on LSD, barking wildly.

'Stay!' the man commands his dogs, as they look longingly after Murphy. He then gives us a real earful about how Murphy shouldn't be off the lead because he is so badly behaved. In the end we just walk off and pretend we can't hear him. It's awful because he carries on shouting for ages while we crash through the trees to get away from him. Murphy has done an impressive runner and is nowhere to be seen.

I'm really tired now, we seem to have walked for miles and breakfast seems an age away. I was so miserable I didn't eat much this morning. Now I feel so stressed I could devour anything.

Finn is cursing under his breath. He tries whistling but there is no sign of Murphy.

When we hear screaming I say immediately, 'Oh no! It must be Murphy. What's he doing now?'

We set off at a run. We have walked round in a big circle and we cut through the trees and come out on to the main bridle path again.

There we find Murphy with an old woman and her two spaniel-type dogs. The spaniels are both really fat and manky looking but Murphy obviously thinks they are the biggest turn on in the world. He is positioned precariously on top of one of them gyrating like a limbo dancer. The old woman is hitting him with a walking stick. As we approach he jumps off the first dog and mounts the other one. The dogs are too fat or too stupid to run away from him—or (heaven forbid) they are actually enjoying his attentions. The old woman is nearly hysterical. She's screaming all this rubbish about how he's killing her dogs. Stupid!

Finn breaks into a sprint. His legs are a lot longer than mine are and he gets to the old woman just as her voice rises in a scream straight from a horror film. Several other dog walkers have been attracted by the noise. And one of them, a florid-faced man in a green padded waistcoat, calls out 'Well done, lad!' to Finn, as Finn throws himself into a rugby tackle and grapples Murphy away from the horrid spaniels.

I arrive breathlessly just as Finn has managed to get the choke chain around Murphy's neck.

The old woman and the other dog walker—the man—are both talking at once. Well, they're shouting really.

'You want to get that dog under control, lad. He's a danger to the public.'

'I've a good mind to call the police. That dog shouldn't be allowed to roam the woods doing such things . . . ' the old woman screams.

'You shouldn't have your dogs out if they're in season,' Finn says. I am busy helping him hold on to the lead. What Murphy really needs is a straitjacket.

'I'll have you know they are not in season! My girls have both been seen to. And that dog needs seeing to. I've a good mind to call the police and report you for having a dangerous dog running loose.'

'Oh yeah,' Finn says coolly. 'Call 999 and tell them about an attempted dog rape. The police haven't got anything more important to worry about.'

'Don't you dare speak to me like that! You yob!' she shrills.

'We don't want your sort around here. Clear off back to where you came from!' the man says nastily. 'I've got my mobile phone with me. I can have the police here in minutes,' he adds importantly.

Murphy suddenly gives up the fight. He stops pulling and barking and flops down in a heap. I am terrified. 'Finn!' I wail. 'He's hurt! I think he's dying! She's hurt him with the walking stick.'

'Come along, dear,' the man says to the old woman solicitously. 'I'll walk you back to your car. You've had a nasty shock.'

Finn is on his knees next to Murphy, feeling his head, ribs, and limbs. His hands moving swiftly yet gently. When he has finished Murphy raises his head and sighs, looking up at Finn with loving eyes.

I stand up and scream at the retreating backs of the old woman and the man. 'If you've hurt my dog I'll report you to the police and the RSPCA and my father will take you to court! You fecking bastards!' I'm crying too much to care what I say.

Finn stands up and puts his arm around me. 'He's OK, I'm nearly sure of it. Look—he's got up now. I think he's just exhausted. She wasn't hitting him hard. He didn't appear to notice and anyway he's got a great thick coat for protection. I've checked him all over and he hasn't flinched or whined once. He's not in pain.'

Murphy is on his feet and stretching. He is panting and grinning up at me with his tongue lolling. He does a few sideways steps and wags his tail.

'Well, that was a bravura performance,' Finn says to Murphy. 'Playing the old soldier like that. You're not half as stupid as you look.'

I'm on my knees in the mud with my arms around Murphy's neck. 'Is he really OK?' I sob. 'I thought he was going to die.'

'Let's walk him slowly back to the van, if he's limping or doesn't seem OK, I promise we'll find a vet. But he's been running amok for hours—he must be busted by now.' Finn puts his hand under my elbow and pulls me to my feet. 'Have you got a hanky?' he asks kindly, and it's then I realize that I've been crying so hard my face is wet with snot and tears. I find a tissue in my pocket and blow my nose.

'Those people were so tight. What was that stupid man going on about—"we don't want your sort around here"—does he think he owns the world?' I grumble.

'Oh, don't take any notice. If you wear a bike jacket and your hair is the wrong length you get it all the time,' Finn says.

'What do you do when people are like that?' I ask curiously. Up until now most people I've met have been nice to me. I'm unused to aggression from total strangers.

'Ignore it. I don't live my life to please them. I dress as I choose.'

We walk slowly back to the van. Murphy lopes next to

us, loose-limbed as a beanie baby. He seems quite grateful to jump up into the van (we don't need the piece of cold chicken I had brought along as a bribe). He lies down on his blanket with a sigh, stretches himself out and goes to sleep immediately.

It's only then that I realize I am shaking all over and I feel sick. I look down at my clothes and then across at Finn. We are both covered in mud, dog slobber, and ditch water. My jeans are soaking wet and clinging to my legs.

There is a chapter in Mum's helpful little book entitled 'Your First Date—How to Handle it'. Somehow I don't think I'm going to bother to read it.

'Shall we go back to my house and get cleaned up?' I suggest. 'And I'll cook us something to eat?'

'Will your folks be OK about that?' Finn asks. I try to nod brightly but for some reason he sees right through my pretence.

'You didn't tell them you were coming out with me, did you?' he says, looking straight at me.

It seems pointless to lie. I shake my head. 'It's not because of you . . . ' I say lamely. 'They're all upset because of some big family secret that your mum knows about. It's all really silly because I've worked out what it is and it doesn't matter at all to me. I mean, what difference does it make if Dad's mother was a junkie? It just doesn't matter. I don't know why they think it's such a big deal.'

It's weird because I see his face change and a shiver, colder than anything I've ever felt, starts deep inside me. 'It's not that, is it? It's something else and you know what it is?'

He looks away, but I have seen the expression in his eyes. It's weird because it's taken years for me to know what Jack is thinking—but with Finn it's like an instinct. He can't hide anything from me.

'You do know—don't you?'

'No . . . ' he says. I am so certain he is lying I can't find the energy to argue with him. I curl up in the seat, trying to get warm. I'd thought losing Jack was the most terrible thing that could happen to me. Now I am scared because suddenly I know there is worse to come. So I pretend to look out of the window, but really I am just hiding my face from Finn. Hot slow tears slide down my cheeks and I am too tired and sad to wipe them away.

# 10

My hands are shaking so much I can hardly get the gates open at home. I am as cold and wet and miserable as a half-drowned kitten and my brain feels like scrambled eggs.

'Would you like to come in for a coffee?' I ask Finn, glancing at his stern profile. I suppose in the back of my mind is the idea that if I get him into the house I might be able to make him tell me what he knows. But it's more than that. The idea of him leaving makes me feel miserable. It's as if being in his company is necessary for my happiness.

'No, thanks,' he says shortly. 'I'll get home and get these films developed for you. I'll drop them round later on.'

I know I've made a big mistake by not telling my parents I was going out with him. He thinks I'm ashamed of him or something awful like that. I don't know what I can say to make things better.

'Thanks a lot for everything,' I gulp, avoiding looking at him.

'Will you be all right?' he asks.

'Yes, I'll be fine,' I lie.

'See you then,' he says.

And I am left in a heap in the utility room with a muddy Murphy and my mind going round like a hamster on a wheel.

Waiting makes time move slowly. I wait for my parents to tell me whatever the secret is and I wait to see Finn again. I am disappointed in both these things.

There are loads of times when I think Mum or Dad is going to start talking. There are pauses in endless conversations; frowns, worried looks, sentences half started—but then nothing—and the big wall of silence really gets on my nerves.

Finn obviously doesn't want to see me. He drops the photos round in a big brown envelope and doesn't even bother to ring the bell. I only know it's him who has delivered them because I hear the roar of the bike engine.

The photos are brilliant. It's due to his camera and not my photography. Also he took quite a few shots and they are truly amazing. There's a great one of Murphy and me together that I didn't even know was being taken. I look really happy and almost pretty. This is in direct contrast to how I look and feel at the moment. Depression bites. I can hardly be bothered to get out of bed. And washing my hair seems as difficult as going on an expedition up the Himalayas. I stay in bed until Mum starts muttering about doctor's appointments and tonics. I wish I could tell them what the real problem is and ask them to start talking to me. But to them I am still little Jadey, they can't or won't accept that I've grown up.

Finally I start work on my art project and work so hard that Mum starts nattering about eyestrain and the importance of fresh air and exercise. Honestly, you can't win with parents. She keeps running in with nutritious little snacks for me and talking about keeping my strength up.

The cartoons turn out really well, thanks to the fantastic photos. I get quite excited and I would like to phone Finn and talk to him about what I've done with the photos, and also to thank him properly for helping me, but I am too scared.

Jack is working all the time. He phones and tells me he's saving up so he can go to France for Christmas. 'Xavier has asked me to stay with him and his family,' Jack says shyly. It's a relief in a way not to see him. It's easier to disguise my hurt when talking on the phone.

When I am not drawing I am overwhelmed by anxiety, not just about whatever it is that Mum and Dad need to tell me but also, shamefully, I worry that our friends at school will notice a difference in Jack and me. We have been a couple for so long it seems inconceivable that we could become two separate entities. But things aren't the same—I have changed. I still love Jack but something in my emotional spectrum has altered. It's like when you mix a big blob of white paint on your palette and add it to all the colours you've been using. Superficially everything looks the same but really they are different. And that's how I feel—different: nervy, edgy, not interested in food, obsessed with the photographs and my pictures. I redo the portrait of Finn in pencil and then try it in various different mediums. I use charcoal first of all, then watercolour, and finally acrylic. I have to hide all this from Mum, because I know if she sees endless pictures of Finn she'll be dead suspicious.

Saturday arrives and Dad takes me to *Flower Power*.

'Jade,' he says to me really seriously when we get in the car, 'I want to ask you something.'

'OK,' I say. I am quite breathless with panic. This is it! He's going to tell me!

'I'm going to be starting a new business. Something small and classy—mainly barn and cottage conversions. A couple of the lads, Riaz and Paul, real good workers, want to come in with me. And I wondered if I could use your name. I'd like to call it Jade Homes.'

'I'd take it as a compliment,' I say. I don't know whether I am disappointed or relieved. But I suppose sitting at the traffic lights in the city centre isn't really the appropriate place to discuss family secrets.

There is no sign of Finn at *Flower Power*. And this time I know the emotion I'm experiencing is disappointment. If I'm honest I've been looking forward to seeing him all week. And I've brought my portfolio of cartoons to show him. Now I feel really stupid—like a little kid who takes a spider in a jar to show teacher and finds she's arachnophobic.

Dad disappears upstairs to have coffee with Nola. I hear the hum of their voices and wonder what on earth they find to talk about. I am busy making circles of wire and wadding for the Christmas wreaths. It's hard work and the wire cutter hurts my fingers. Self-pity floods through me.

When Dad eventually comes down he seems preoccupied. 'Nola's got some deliveries at Thistle Hill this afternoon so she'll give you a lift home,' he says as he kisses me goodbye.

Then this amazing little fantasy starts in my head. All about how Finn will come back and offer to do the deliveries just so he can give me a lift and how we will talk . . . This tiny spark of hope sustains me through the afternoon. I try to breathe life into it, like a stone-age cave dweller rubbing sticks and praying for fire, right up until the van is loaded and we are ready to leave.

'Come on, Jade, I must get you home. You're into overtime,' Nola jokes. 'I'll tell Finn how good your pictures are,' she adds kindly.

'Yeah, I've got to take them into school on Monday,' I say miserably.

That's it—the end of hope. A whole week before there's any chance of seeing him. A week—it stretches before me like an eternity. And what will I do if the same thing happens next week and he isn't there? I feel like crying. Instead I just sit in sulky silence in the front of the van. Nola doesn't appear to notice. She talks non-stop anyway. All I have to do is listen.

'How's your lovely boyfriend?' she suddenly asks. That makes me jump.

'Oh Jack . . . ' I say, playing for time. I'd quite like to tell her the truth. I'm sick of deception and lies. But after all it isn't my secret. 'Things are off between us . . . ' I mutter.

'Oh, shame,' Nola says. 'He's got a kind face.'

'He is a very sweet person,' I say stiffly. 'I think he'll always be my best friend.'

'Your dad says he's been like family since you were both tiny. Maybe he's more like your brother,' she says.

'Yes, I think that's it,' I mutter.

'Anyway, don't be in a hurry to grow up. It's a long hard road once you get there,' she says and laughs.

'Would you say thank you to Finn for helping me with the photos,' I say.

'Why don't you give him a ring this evening and thank him yourself,' she says. And I wonder if she thinks it's rude of me to send a message when he has gone to so much trouble.

'OK, I'll do that,' I say miserably.

Because I am terrified of Mum and Dad overhearing I phone him on my mobile from the bathroom with the shower running. 'Hi—it's Jade. I just called to say thanks for the photos—the cartoons have turned out really well.'

'That's good . . . ' (Long silence—obviously neither of us knows what to say.) Finally, as the credit ticks away on my phone, he asks, 'How's Murphy?'

'Fine. I told Mum and Dad about his adventures with the spaniels. Mum says Murphy's got to be castrated and Dad says he's got to go to police dog training classes. I don't know which is going to be the more painful for him.'

Finn laughs. (I can't believe it! I've made Finn laugh! I close my eyes and try to imagine what he looks like when he is laughing.)

'Would you like to take him out tomorrow morning? I know a place with fewer people and no sheep.'

'That would be lovely,' I say, my face is hot and my heart is hammering. (Finn has asked me out! Or has he? Have I just accepted a date on behalf of my dog?)

'Same time,' he says.

'Same place,' I add.

I don't tell Mum and Dad. They are really tense and edgy. They keep on half starting serious-type conversations with me: 'Jade. There is something we need to discuss . . . ' and then chickening out.

When Lucy Holden rings and says a gang from school are going to the cinema I jump at the chance to go out for the evening. Being with my parents is like walking on black ice. I keep waiting for the moment to arrive when my feet disappear from under me and I find myself slithering and sliding into the world of 'the secret'. I've got to the stage now when I don't think I really want to know.

I keep thinking that I've lived happily for sixteen years without this knowledge. So why can't I continue for the rest of my life in blessed ignorance? I have passed through stages when I have been desperate to know what the secret is, but this longing has been like hunger and eventually you get past wanting food and just feel sick. That's how I've got—sick of wondering. I don't want to know now. I don't care any more.

In the morning I get all my walking gear ready in the utility room and wait until Finn arrives before I tell them I am going out.

'But what about your lunch?' Mum asks, as she shoots an anguished look at Dad.

'You can put it in the microwave for me,' I say avoiding their eyes.

'Why didn't you tell us . . . ' Dad starts to ask.

'I'm only taking the dog for a walk. He is meant to be mine!' I snap.

Murphy obviously remembers the good time he had at Farringdon Forest. (Maybe he dreams about the manky spaniels and that's why he twitches and whimpers in his sleep, poor boy!) Anyway he leaps into the back of the van and sits with his tongue lolling looking very pleased with himself.

'Are you OK?' Finn asks, and he looks at me so anxiously I wonder if I should check my face in a mirror in case I've suddenly developed spots. The intensity of his gaze makes me feel uncomfortable and I wish I hadn't put on so much mascara. I've taken loads of trouble over my hair and make-up and suddenly I feel stupid and wish I hadn't.

'I'm fine,' I say breezily. 'I've got loads of biscuits in my pockets. Murphy is on a new training programme. You let him off the lead and keep calling him back. Every time he comes he gets a biscuit. He obviously has some deep-rooted phobia about starvation because he will do anything for a biscuit—well, just about anything.'

'Sounds good,' Finn says.

We travel in silence. I watch his hands and avoid looking at his face because I keep wanting to stare at him and compare him to my portraits.

We drive through the damp fog of the morning out to a landmark called Armsdale Crag. It's a huge outcrop of natural rock, and it rises up out of the moorland mist like a Gothic castle.

We park the van, climb over a stile, and set off across the springy turf. Murphy goes crackers for a bit—racing around like he's in the Grand National.

I peer through the mist. 'You are sure there are no sheep around, aren't you?'

'There are lots in the summer but not now. The farmers move them up to the heather. It's too wet down here—they'd get foot rot.'

We march on in silence—like two soldiers going into battle. Finn seems very glum. I begin to wonder why he's asked us out. It's hard work walking over the boggy grass and there is a nagging cold wind that pinches my face. I'm glad when we get to the crag and can shelter under the great overhang of granite. It's almost like being in a cave. We lean against the rock and get our breath.

Murphy comes and sits down next to us. He's soaking wet and panting like a steam train. I give him a biscuit and stroke his ears.

'Was it OK when they told you? It didn't upset you too much, did it?' Finn suddenly asks.

I stare down at Murphy, playing for time. I realize I

am biting at my lower lip and I try to smile instead. The sharp hunger of wanting to know the secret is back, just as your appetite returns when you smell bacon cooking.

'What did you expect me to do—detonate?' I ask.

'I don't know. I mean, it's never bothered me not knowing who my father is . . . but it really bugs some people. Nola's always going on about medical records but I don't give a stuff about all that.'

Too late do I realize what I have done. I have laid a trap for him and now I don't like what I have seized. For a moment I tremble—then I look straight at him and say, 'You'd better explain fully because they haven't told me anything.'

He swears—some of those ripe St Aidan's-type swear words that he must have learnt when he played football. I wince. 'Why didn't you tell me? Why did you just let me go blabbing on?' he says, and I see that he is either angry or upset—or maybe a mixture of both.

'Because I thought you might say something which would give me a clue what it is all about. And you did . . . ' To my shame my eyes fill and my chin trembles.

Finn swears again, but more softly, and he reaches out his arms and pulls me close to him.

'How can he not be my dad?' I ask brokenly, burying my head against his leather jacket.

'Your mam was pregnant when she met him. They fell in love and Rick didn't mind that you belonged to someone else. That's the kind of guy he is.'

'I don't belong to anyone else—I belong to him,' I say with a sob.

'Yes—of course you do,' Finn says gently. 'But not biologically. And for some reason your parents think you should know that.'

'How come you and Nola know the truth?'

'Your mam and Nola were best friends at school. Your mam stuck up for Nola when she got pregnant. Even though your gran went ape. Your mam knitted baby clothes and used to go to the hospital with Nola and stuff like that. Nola says she wouldn't have got through it all without her. So when your mam was in the same kind of trouble she phoned Nola. Then you came to live with us. We're the only people who know. Nola was worried you might be upset. That's why she wanted me to talk to you.'

I pull away from him. He asked me out because his mother told him to! I feel a total failure.

'Who was this person. The person who . . . '

'You know your mam was a nanny? Well, the family she worked for took a villa in Spain for August. She met a Spanish boy. They fell in love—but then he refused to accept she was pregnant. He didn't believe her.'

'Didn't believe her!' I say angrily. 'How absolutely stupid.' I pull away from him. His face is really embarrassed. 'Why didn't he believe her?'

He doesn't answer. I am suddenly furious. 'For goodness' sake, Finn. You can't tell me this much and then get squeamish. She must have told Nola. And Nola's bound to have told you.'

'She doesn't have anyone else to talk to,' Finn says defensively. 'She hasn't told anyone but me. She told me in confidence and only because she thought I might be able to help you.'

'What, hold my hand and give me a hanky? Oh, what a good lad who does just what his mummy tells him. Were you a Boy Scout, by any chance? Have you come prepared with a box of Kleenex?' My voice is sneering. I am hurt and I want him to be hurt too. I'm like an injured dog that bites the person who tries to help.

I get hold of his arm and if he wasn't so much bigger than me I would shake him with exasperation. 'Tell me— it's my life story, not yours, it isn't fair that you know and I don't.'

Finn doesn't meet my eyes. 'They had sex once—on the beach—they'd had too much to drink. Your mam said she didn't think they'd gone all the way but they must have done. The boy said he hadn't . . . you know. Oh fecking hell, Jade. I shouldn't be telling you all this. It's so personal. How would your mam feel if she knew?'

I bury my face in my hands. I do this partly to block out his face—so full of pity and pain—and also to hide my grief. God! All the sex education we had at school never prepared me for this. Is it possible to have sex and not know you've done it? How young and stupid were they? It's gross—the worst thing he's told me. I mean if they'd been in love and going at it like rabbits every night at least that would have been normal. But to be conceived by mistake in a drunken fumble when neither of them knew what was happening is absolutely awful.

He puts his arms around me. He continues—maybe it is a relief to tell it all. 'She was upset the day she met your dad. She'd had a letter from the boy saying she must be mistaken and he didn't want anything more to do with her. She was crying and your dad's never been able to bear anyone crying.'

'They were all crying. Felix, the baby, and poor Mum . . . ' I say with a sniff.

'It may not have been the best start in life,' Finn says. 'But no baby could have been more wanted—I promise you. They adored you—we all did. It was like the first Christmas when you were born. I can still remember it.'

Finn pulls me into an enormous hug but Murphy—jealous of our closeness—leans against my back and tries to lick my hair. Finn pushes him off and we start the long walk back to the van. Finn holds my hand. I wish I could take my glove off so I could feel his hand properly but I am too shy.

'I don't think I can bear my parents telling me the truth. It will just be so awful hearing it from them,' I lament. 'What can I do?'

'I don't know. Rick's been talking to Nola and he said he was definitely going to tell you last night.'

'I went out to the cinema . . . ' I say miserably.

'Nola's been saying it's right for him to tell you. She's a great one for getting things out in the open. But if I tell her what's happened maybe she'll be able to talk him out of it.'

'Did she tell you all about your father?' I ask. I feel him tense and when I glance at him I sense pain in his eyes.

'Yes, and I will tell you about him, but not now, not today.'

'OK,' I say, rather hurt that he won't confide in me.

We get back to the stile and Murphy, who has been so good up to now, suddenly gets skittish and won't come to us. He dances and prances, coming close and then moving away just as our hands are about to take hold of his collar. Not even a biscuit will tempt him.

We run around in circles until I feel sweat trickling down my back. Great date this has turned out to be. Crying and perspiring. I'm sure Mum's little book doesn't recommend either.

Finn stops and curses softly. Then he says, 'Come on—we're going back to the van. You get into the driver's seat and turn the engine on.'

'What are you going to do?' I ask breathlessly.

'Catch this dog. He thinks he's so smart. Well, he's not, and I'm going to show him,' Finn adds grimly.

'What happens if another car comes into the car park?' I say anxiously.

'Don't worry, I'll get him before he gets near any cars,' Finn says. He looks really fierce—his eyes are narrow and glittering.

I get into the van and Finn crouches out of sight. As soon as Murphy hears the engine he leaps over the stile like a winner in the Grand National and Finn leaps on him, moving with the speed of an Apache warrior. He grabs Murphy's collar and clips on the lead. Then he opens the van door. 'Get in,' he commands.

Murphy looks a bit miffed at being ambushed, but he jumps up and moves down the van as if he will lick my face.

'Sit down, now!' Finn snaps. Murphy sits and grins at me. 'He's a real nuisance,' Finn grumbles.

'He is improving, honestly. He can be left on his own now,' I say, trying to sound bright.

'He needs more than improving.' Finn wipes his face and scowls. It's awful when he's cross, like a storm blowing in from the sea and turning day to night.

By the look of things there won't be any more invitations for Murphy. And I sit hunched and miserable looking out of the van window and trying not to cry, because this sad fog-filled day suddenly seems like the end of everything.

# 11

When I get home I find the last person in the world I want to see waiting for me—Sybil. She's in the kitchen, standing just a bit too close to Jack for his comfort and mine. Mum says apologetically, 'I bumped into Jack as he was leaving work and asked him if he wanted to come back and have some supper. And then, what a surprise, we met Sybil too! Wasn't that a lovely coincidence?' Mum questions anxiously.

I suspect that the subtext to this is that Sybil was hanging around the supermarket waiting for Jack to finish work. She's such a stalker—it's really tight to spook him like this. Poor Jack!

'So we'll all have supper together—shall we?' Mum suggests.

I grin and nod with enthusiasm. (What else can I do?) At least it means an evening when Mum and Dad will not be able to talk to me about the past. I give Jack a hug, because he looks so pinched and miserable. 'Wait until you see my art project. It's wicked,' I tell him.

'Jadey has worked so hard,' Mum says. 'I got quite worried. She would hardly stop to eat. But she's finished it and it's lovely. We're so proud of her.' Mum rattles away for a bit, telling Sybil all about my pictures. I am rather touched because Mum can describe each one in detail even down to the colours I've used. Sybil's eyes are glazed with boredom as she eats through a bowl of crisps Mum has put out on the table. The good thing about Mum cataloguing my work is that it makes her relax a bit. But I am aware that Dad is staring at me and I sense panic behind his eyes, or is this just my imagination? I put my arms around his neck and give him a mega-hug.

'Murphy was brilliant. A little tiny tantrum right at the end of the walk but the rest of the time he came back like an angel. Your training is working like a charm. Haven't I got a clever old daddy? We'll be able to get you a job in the circus next.'

It's pitiful how happy all this banter makes him. I take Sybil and Jack off to my room with some nibbles and cans of Coke because I don't think I can keep this pretence up for too long.

When I was a little girl I had a book called *Would you rather?* It was full of daft things like 'Would you rather eat a plate of worms or a country pancake?' and 'Would you rather your dad did a highland fling at school or your mum had a row in a shoe shop?' There were some really brilliant illustrations and Dad and I loved reading it— although I suspect that Mum found it a bit gross. I am reminded of this book because this evening the choice seems to be 'Would you rather spend an evening stuck in your bedroom with a sulky Jack and a sly Sybil or would you rather talk to your parents about their misspent youth?' I feel so desperate I toy with the idea of raiding Dad's drinks cupboard for a shot or two of vodka, because I don't really know how am I going to get through the next few hours.

'What a gorgeous room!' Sybil says, marching around my room and picking my personal things up and inspecting them. (I think this is really rude, but I don't say anything—what's the point?) 'I'd kill for a room like this,' she adds. 'It must be the master bedroom. It's got an en suite! How come you get to have it?'

'Because I have a desk and all my school stuff in here . . . It's meant to be where I study.'

'But your mother lets you use the dining room,' she challenges me.

I don't really know why I have to discuss our domestic arrangements with Sybil. Ignoring her I pull out my portfolio and start to show Jack my pictures.

'All your subjects are easy ones,' Sybil says, butting in. 'There's nothing to drawing a few pictures or slapping a bit of paint about, is there? It's kids' stuff.'

Then she starts going on about her subjects—further maths and science—and really showing off. Jack and I sit silently and let her natter away. 'Of course,' she says to Jack, 'you're taking music and that's quite a good subject to have, isn't it? I'm surprised you don't play an instrument, Jade. Didn't Mummy and Daddy send their little princess to music and ballet lessons?'

'Actually we weren't that well off when I was little—anyway I'm tone deaf and I hate dancing so there wouldn't have been much point them scrimping and saving.'

'Oh! So you haven't always lived in a luxurious palace?' she says with a giggle.

'No.' Just for a split second I am tempted to tell her that we lived above a shop on the St Aidan's estate just to see if I can wipe the silly smile off her face. But for some reason I can't say it. I feel strange. I want to keep Finn and that part of my life a secret. For some reason it would be unbearable to have it ridiculed by bitchy Sybil.

'It wouldn't matter where we lived or how much money we had—we'd still be a happy family,' I say. And I see her mouth tighten and know that I've hit home with that remark.

I put MTV on really loudly and Jack and I settle down on the bed together to watch. There are two chairs so Sybil can take her pick. I have the volume on so high it's impossible to talk over it. Sybil shouts, 'Digital TV too. No expense spared!' I just grin and nod. She's such a cow. I know she thinks I'm spoilt to death. (She and Nana would get on great, I'm convinced of it.) But why the hell should it matter to me?

Jack is really clingy. Honestly, you'd think I was a mother kangaroo and he the little joey. I have the feeling that if he could he would climb right inside my jumper to get away from Sybil.

After a bit Sybil gets restless. She roves the room. Any minute I expect her to start opening my drawers and researching my underwear. Then she comes across and perches on the edge of the bed. First she reaches for the remote and turns the volume down low, then she takes hold of Jack's foot and slides her hand up over his ankle. 'I'm lonely, is there room for three on the bed?' she wheedles in this horrible fake little-girl voice. 'Can I come and have a cuddle too? Might it be more fun with three?'

She moves as if she will stretch herself next to Jack, moving like a cat on the prowl. I open my mouth to protest but I am too late. Jack jerks his foot with all the thrust of a bad tempered mule and swears at her. He must have caught her off balance because she flies off the bed and collides with my bedside bureau.

Jack is up on his feet, standing over Sybil who is lying face down on the carpet like a cartoon character who has just been thrown through a window by a bomb. 'Just leave me alone, you effing bitch. I don't want anything to do with you. You repulse me. You don't understand anything do you? You are just so thick. Well—go away and work out this little mathematical equation. One—I'm gay. Two—I love Jade and always have done. Three—I want nothing to do with you or any other girl. Now,' he snarls, 'you don't have to be a further maths scholar to work out the effing answer—just leave me alone!' He leans right over her and hisses into the back of her head. 'Got it?'

Sybil rolls slowly over on to her back. I gasp in horror and Jack moves back from her quickly. She must have cut her lip or bitten it as she fell. Blood streaks her chin and drips down on to her cream roll-neck.

'I'm bleeding,' she announces dramatically.

'Oh, for heaven's sake,' I say crossly, rushing into the bathroom and soaking a towel. 'Put something cold on it. It'll soon stop.'

Jack has thrown himself face down on the bed. He lies so still he could be dead. No help there! I try to clean the carpet, Sybil's jumper, and stem the flow of blood from her busted lip.

'Don't say anything to my parents,' I beg. 'Please. Look, we'll just say we were dancing and messing around and you tripped.'

Just at that moment Dad shouts up the stairs that supper is ready. I find Sybil a clean jumper and throw it at her. Her lip is pretty swollen and her expression is venomous. 'It's roast beef and Yorkshire pudding. I should miss the horseradish if I were you,' I add.

'Very funny,' she mutters. Then she asks: 'Was it true what he said?' I don't answer. But she must be able to see the truth in my eyes. She says, 'Oh,' and dabs at her mouth.

I go and shake Jack's shoulder. 'Just come downstairs and have something to eat. The parents are in a stress at the moment anyway. All this might throw them over the edge. Please, Jack, for me. Come and have some supper.'

He must be able to hear the desperation in my voice, because he gets off the bed and pushes his hair out of his eyes. Then he and Sybil follow me downstairs.

We sit around the table, avoiding looking at each other. Mum is busy dishing up. No one speaks or mentions Sybil's lip. My brain feels numb. I can't seem to remember what we talk about at meal times normally. Dad is carving the joint, Mum is fussing, and the silence grows ever longer.

I open my mouth and start to talk. (And thank God for Murphy.) I start at the beginning—pretending that Sybil will be really interested in Murphy's story. I hardly stop to eat. I make everyone laugh when I describe the meeting with the spaniels. And by the end of the meal

I am absolutely exhausted. I feel like a stand-up comedienne who has just finished a tough show.

'No pudding for me,' I croak.

'I think you're starting with a cold, Jadey,' Mum says with a frown, 'you're very flushed.'

'I'm fine. I think I'll just have an early night. We've got to display our art projects first thing tomorrow morning so I've got to get in early.'

Saying I need an early night works like a charm on the parents. Dad takes Jack and Sybil home and I flee up to my room. When Mum comes in to see me I pretend to be asleep. She tiptoes in, kisses me, and whispers, 'I love you, sweetheart,' and then creeps out. That makes me cry. I cry because I feel sorry for Mum and Dad, and because I feel sorry for myself. I cry because I'm confused about Finn, miserable about Jack, and heartbroken about Dad. I know I ought to be thinking of how to sort all these problems out. But I really am tired and before I can get my head around any solutions I fall asleep.

I am into school really early but Jack is there before me. He doesn't look as if he has slept and there are dark shadows under his beautiful eyes. 'I've nearly finished displaying my work, I'll give you a hand with yours,' he says.

When we are alone behind the screens he gives me a hug and whispers, 'I love you, Jade.' And I hug him back. 'Do you think Sybil will tell people?' he asks, his voice agonized.

'Sybil's name has been mud since her wonderful party, no one will take any notice of what she says. I think most people realize she's a screwball by now,' I say reassuringly. 'Just ignore her.'

When Mr Garforth comes into the hall he is rendered speechless by my work. His mouth opens so wide with shock he nearly cracks his jaw on the floor. I have enough pictures to fill four boards and they look mega-impressive mounted on black paper. (Even when I'm being modest it's obvious to me that they're nearly as good as Jack's work.)

I've never seen any teacher so surprised. 'This is very impressive, Jade,' he manages to say at last. 'That last little adrenalin rush over half term seems to have worked, but do try to work more consistently next time.'

'I wonder what he would have said to Van Gogh?' I whisper to Jack and manage to make him smile.

While we are having lunch, and Jack is telling me how brilliant I am, I say, 'Well—I wouldn't have got it done without Finn. He's been great.'

'You're quite keen on him, aren't you? You won't let him mess you around will you, Jade. He seems quite—' Jack stops; before he can continue I turn on him furiously.

'Don't say Finn's rough, because he isn't!' I whisper angrily. 'He's . . . He's . . . ' A great wave of emotion submerges all the words in my brain. 'He's nice . . . ' I say lamely. (NICE! What kind of a compliment is that?)

'I just don't want you to get hurt,' Jack says miserably. 'I love you to bits, Jadey, I want to look after you. If any bloke messes you around I'll kill him.'

I can't speak. My mind is reeling. I am seeing my life over the last few weeks as if a film is playing out before me. I swoop down like a camera and review the times Finn and I have been together and the truth hits me like a slap across the face. I'm in love. I have been for weeks, but have been too dim and obsessed with Jack to be able to recognize it. That doesn't worry me too much. OK, I've been really stupid but at least I've seen the light now. What does concern me is the big question—how can I make Finn love me?

I am short, I am not really pretty (apart from in Finn's photos), I still look as if I am about twelve. I am three years younger than Finn is—and it seems like eons not years. He remembers me when I was a baby and thinks of me as a little kid. Worst of all I have insulted him on a fairly regular basis whereas he has been really good to me.

'He doesn't think of me like that . . . ' I say brokenly to Jack.

'He's asked you out, hasn't he?' Jack says. 'Why would he do that . . . '

'Nola asked him to take me out. I can't explain why now. But it's all hopeless. It's not that he'll hurt me. I've hurt myself. My heart is broken and I've never even kissed him. I'm just a total failure.'

Looking down at my lunch I realize my appetite has gone. I push my plate away.

'How could anyone not love you?' Jack whispers, touching my hand with his fingertips. It's such a sweet thing to say my eyes fill with tears. We are so absorbed in our little world of worry that it takes us a second to realize that our names are coming over the tannoy system. We are being asked by Big Willie to return to the main hall.

'Oh, don't say we've lost the staple gun,' I mutter furiously. 'Garforth's such an old woman about his equipment.'

Mr Garforth meets us in the doorway. The hall is crowded with people and there is tension in the air, an electric atmosphere like when there's a fight in the playground. Something is up.

'A terrible thing has happened,' Mr Garforth says to us. He's really upset. 'In all my years of teaching I've never had to contend with anything like this . . . Clear off!' he yells to the crowds. They take no more notice of him than if he had been a bluebottle buzzing against the window. 'Get off to the lunch room, immediately, or it will be detention for all of you,' he shrieks. Still everyone ignores him. But the crowd seems to register Jack and me. As we move into the hall, with Mr Garforth hovering next to us like an anxious chicken, squawking and flapping, the kids silently move out of the way. It's a bit like when the Red Sea parted for Moses. It's seriously scary.

'Come and get your work down immediately. I will fetch a dustbin,' Mr Garforth is saying to us.

The last few kids move out of the way and then I know why we need a dustbin.

'What the hell?' Jack cries out, but I don't speak. I feel a shiver go down my back, as if something evil has crawled down my spine.

While we have been at lunch someone has taken a can of spray paint and scrawled on Jack's work and mine. That alone would have been bad enough. But the big black words written up there for the whole world to see are really shocking. I did not know that there were so many horrible ways to say that someone is gay.

Jack immediately begins to drag his work off the screens but I am too shocked for a moment to move. Numbly I stare at my lovely pictures and the precious photos I took with Finn's camera. Every single one has 'fag-hag' scrawled over it. The paint is still wet. It drips down onto the shiny wood of the floor like thick black drops of poison.

With a gasp of sheer horror I start to help Jack tear his work down; my fingers claw at paper and staples until they are raw. But I don't care about that. I can't bear for people to see this violation, and read all that awful stuff about Jack. Jack is crying, but I am beyond any kind of emotion. I am as hard and cold as marble. Something inside me tells me I can't afford to cry. I need to be calm and strong. Because someone has got to look after Jack.

# 12

When finally we get the screens clear there is an eerie silence in the hall. The crowds have left. Mr Garforth says, 'Go to Mrs Williams's office, now.' Just as if we are the culprits or are in some kind of trouble.

Jack just bolts out of the hall. He doesn't take his school bag, his blazer, or anything. He just runs. I drop everything and tear after him, ignoring the entreaties of Mr Garforth. The kids in the corridors move out of the way as Jack careers out of the school like a maniac.

It's sleeting outside. I at least have my jumper on. Jack is wearing only his shirt. I suppose he is running so hard he hasn't noticed the arctic wind or the sharp stabs of ice against his face. I try to shout at him to stop and wait for me but my voice is drowned out by the noise of the traffic. Jack runs straight across the road without looking—a couple of cars brake and skid to avoid him. There is a blaring of horns and someone leans out of a van and yells abuse.

That's when I give up shouting. He's not going to stop for me or for anything else—I save myself for running and trying to keep up with him. He is heading away from the city centre, cutting down narrow side streets—at least, thankfully, there is less traffic here. There is no reason for him to make off in this direction. It's not taking us to his home or mine. The randomness of it is terrifying.

Then I lose him. One moment I have him in my sight, the next minute he's gone. I stop, and it's only then I realize that I have a terrible pain in my chest and my breath is rasping in my throat. I stare around completely dazed and disorientated. I had placed all my faith in my ability to keep up with him. It never occurred to me that I would lose him. If I could I would wail and scream out his name but I don't have the strength for that. I tell myself not to panic and I try to keep walking—but now I have stopped running my legs have gone weak and I hobble as if I am a hundred years old.

I look around at the high walls of the factories and mills. Most are derelict and the whole area is strangely silent. Then I spot a narrow cobbled ginnel tucked away at the side of a mill. I have been here before—with Jack. This is a short cut to Underborough. In a split second I know where Jack has gone. I stumble along as fast as I can until the mills give way to residential streets, narrow rows of houses that run in steps down the hillside. This road leads up the steepest hill in the city and I know suddenly that I cannot make it to the top. I grip hold of a streetlight post and wonder what to do. My body is out of control—my legs refuse to move—hysterical thoughts begin to surface in my mind—I will go crazy if I don't find Jack.

I watch an elderly couple come out of a terraced house and carefully lock the door, then they unlock their car. I stagger up to them.

'Excuse me . . . ' I manage to whisper. 'Please could you give me a lift to the top of the hill. I need to get to the cemetery urgently. Underborough Cemetery . . . '

'Go away, clear off,' the man says hurriedly. 'Get in quick, Margaret,' he says to his wife. 'It's come to something when you can't step out of your own front door . . . ' the rest of his grumble is lost to me.

Desperately I turn to the woman—she has grey hair and a kind face. 'Please . . . you are my only hope. Don't turn your back on me. My friend's in trouble. I need to get to the cemetery quickly.'

'Get in, Margaret,' the man says again. 'I know all about this sort. If you let them in the car they pull a knife on you. She's probably on drugs. Don't just stand there, get in the car.'

The woman tuts and shakes her head. 'She's only a little lass, and where would she be keeping a knife?' she says softly. 'Look at her, John. She's only got her school woolly on—and no coat when it's nearly snowing. We'll pop her in the car,' she adds soothingly. 'It'll only take two minutes to take her up the hill.' The woman opens the back door of the car and shoos me in. There is surly silence from the man.

'Thank you, thank you,' I mutter to my good Samaritan.

About halfway up the hill the cemetery comes into view; the smoke blackened monuments and crypts make strange geometric shapes against the barren winter skyline. Jack loves the cemetery. When we did our GCSE projects he spent hours up there sketching stone angels and unusual gravestones. All the old wool barons and mill owners who made the city famous are buried there. In death, as in life, they tried to outdo each other with elaborate stonework and vast memorials to their wealth. I hate the place. Right at the very top of the graveyard is a cenotaph and the most glorious panoramic view of the city. Jack used to say to me, 'It makes me feel as if I can fly when I stand up here.'

In the few short seconds it takes for the car to reach the gates of the cemetery I say a prayer that I will find him there. I dash from the car, mumbling my thanks, because I can see a white shape moving in a desolate zigzag among the dark graves. It is Jack. I am not far behind him.

He makes it to the cenotaph before me. I find him lying on the snowy ground and already the falling flakes are turning his golden hair to silver.

'Jack . . . Jack, you can't stay here. You'll freeze to death.' I try to turn him over. His face is coloured starkly—white skin tinged with blue with terrible streaks of red around his eyes and nose.

'Leave me alone, I'm going to stay here forever,' he mutters. 'Down among the dead men, that's where I deserve to be.'

I pull at him quite roughly. Now I have stopped moving I realize how cold I am. 'You can't stay here,' I argue. Then I begin to shout and swear at him, but he won't do anything but lie on the cold ground and mutter nonsense.

My mobile is in my bag which is lying on the floor in the school hall—but fortunately Jack's phone is in his pocket. He has hardly any credit left but I try to get hold of Dad. His phone rings and rings—but he's not answering. I try Mum but her phone is switched off. Fear makes me shake. If I can't get someone to come and help me I shall have to call 999 and I dread doing that.

Then I think of Nola. She's kind and sensible and will understand. Frowning with concentration I try to remember the number of the shop. If I get a wrong number I'm stuck because the credit will have gone.

When a deep voice answers I have a panic. Then with a flood of relief I realize that it's Finn. 'I'm at Underborough Cemetery. I need you to come now. Bring a blanket. I'm at the top by the . . . ' Then the phone cuts off. I cry then. Hot tears brought on by despair and hearing Finn's voice.

I don't know if he even knew it was me. He might have thought it was a nutter and won't do anything. I pull Jack up into a sitting position—then I slap his face as hard as I can. 'Get up,' I shout.

'Jade,' he opens his eyes and looks at me. 'Go away and leave me alone.'

'I'm not going anywhere without you. Now get up, please.' I manage to get my shoulder into his armpit and push him up on to his feet. And all the time I'm talking— because I can't stand the silence of this place.

'No phone, no credit, no bloody coat,' I shout, as if defying the ghosts to come near and attempt to take Jack away from me. 'We're stuck here with a load of stiffs in the stinking snow. For crying out loud, Jack. Move it. If you want to die like a Brontë I'll find you a sofa and a coal fire. But please can we get out of this place—it's giving me the creeps.' And then I'm ranting all kinds of rubbish. Raving on about how, if the Victorians were so clever and scientific, they didn't get real and cremate people instead of wasting all this space with graves. And all the time I'm slowly edging him along, leading him down the hill as if he's sightless and lame, one arm around his back the other hand wiping snow from his face.

Finn meets us halfway. He's jogging over the grass with a blanket in his arms. He doesn't ask questions or waste time. He wraps the blanket around Jack. Then he takes off his leather jacket and puts it on me, sliding my arms down into the sleeves as if I'm a toddler. Together we half carry half drag Jack down the hill and lay him in the back of the van as if we are grave robbers. Poor Jack is like a zombie. I pray that it's only the effects of the cold and running so far. He has such a wonderful mind—it's full of lovely things and poetry—but like so much in the world that's beautiful it's also worryingly fragile.

Finn is great. He acts as if it's quite normal to be rescuing people from the cemetery, taking them home, finding them clean clothes and making coffee and toast. When we are all warm and dry in the kitchen and Jack is looking human again he says casually, 'When we first got back I phoned your school. Spoke to Mrs Williams—told her you were OK.'

'I can't ever go back there,' Jack says miserably. 'Everyone knows. I can't bear it.' His eyes fill with tears.

Finn says, 'I should just tough it out if I were you, mate. Sex, religion, and politics are your own affair. It's only someone else's business if you are trying to convert them or sell your point of view. I don't wear a badge saying I'm a Catholic. It's private. Tell them all to get stuffed if they ask you anything.'

'It's Sybil who should be hounded out, not you,' I add. 'It'll be OK if we stick together.'

Then I turn to Finn and say a bit apologetically, 'People say awful things . . . ' just in case he thinks Jack is being a wimp.

'Yeah—I know. When I was at school we used "spastic" or "spazzer" as an insult and then one day this new kid started screaming and crying and it turns out his sister is handicapped and it's killing him every time we say it. After that some of the kids said it all the more to taunt him. Some of us tried to stop but, to be honest, those words didn't mean that much to us. But the kid never cried again or seemed to let it worry him. And I wondered what had changed and when I asked him he said, "When they say it I just think that it's better I hear it than Sarah does and it's like I'm protecting her." And I thought—nice one—don't let the bastards grind you down.'

Now to be honest, if I was in Jack's position, I don't think that story would cheer me up very much. But it seems to work like magic on him. He brightens up and even manages to smile at us. It must be some kind of a lad thing that I don't understand.

Dad comes to collect us and I don't have a chance to speak to Finn on my own or to thank him properly. I think it's this that tips the balance and finally upsets me because by the time we get home I am so weepy that Mum makes me lie down on the settee. Jack's mother is away at a sales conference and so he stays here with us. Mum runs around with meals on trays and fusses us until Dad says he's going to change her name to Florence Nightingale.

Jack's OK. He talks to Mum and Dad about what happened, which is important because it means he's facing up to it. I'm confident Finn rescued us in time and Jack will come through this. As for me—I've got chilblains and the worst broken heart in the world. I find myself counting up the hours until I am likely to see Finn again. And every time the phone rings I am up like a clockwork frog scattering cushions and blankets and hot drinks all over the floor, just in case by some miracle it's him.

'If you don't relax, Jade, I'm going to have to phone the doctor and ask for something for you,' Mum says anxiously, handing me another cup of calming herbal tea. I can't sit still or concentrate on anything—not even the soaps on the telly. I can't get a sentence out because my mouth doesn't seem connected to my brain. I feel like screaming that I don't need drugs—all I need is to talk to Finn. What's the matter with me? I had no idea that love was so close to madness.

Dad makes us go into school the following day, even though neither Jack nor I really feel like it. 'Putting things off just makes them worse, not better. Believe me. I know,' Dad says, and there is real misery in his eyes. I feel terrible because I know he is thinking about the secret and I wish I could take all that pain away from him but I don't know how to start to tell them that I know.

School isn't too bad. Everyone is very careful and tiptoes around us as if we are surrounded by landmines. I wonder how long it will take for them to talk to us normally again. The only person who is seriously weird is The Frog, who talks to Jack without looking at him. Mr Garforth gives us an extension for our artwork and Jack begins to plan a new project.

'Oh—go back to the animal shelter, we might get a brother or sister for Murphy,' I tease him.

Jack shakes his head. 'Do you remember how easy life was before the summer holidays?' he says sadly. 'Everything I've touched since then has gone wrong. Talk about King Midas in reverse!'

'Look, don't talk like that!' I say, hugging him hard. (And I don't care if The Frog catches us and thinks we are having sex—maybe I'll lend her Mum's book. That should put her right.) 'You mustn't look back all the time. You have to think about tomorrow and the day after that. Things are fine.'

'Your parents are very edgy, maybe it's me . . . ' he begins anxiously.

'Look—it's not to do with you, it's to do with them. I will tell you about it—but not now. To be honest I think they've known the truth about us for ages and it hasn't mattered a bit to them.'

Edgy doesn't get close to describing the stress Mum and Dad are in. They spend ages whispering in their bedroom and Mum is constantly in tears. A couple of times I think Dad has been crying too and it breaks me up to see him like that. I try to think of some way to make things better for them. It's terrible to know they are unhappy and not be able to help them.

Gloom—and too much work—settles over me like a fog. I paint a really horrible picture in oils. (It's so gruesome it makes the dying saint from Sybil's house look like a comic.) It is an abstract depicting birth. I use lots of scarlet and black and the imagery of a dark tunnel. Mr Garforth gets really excited about it. (What a sad life that man leads.) He says it's a picture full of symbolism and is a giant step forward for me. I'm glad someone likes it. I daren't show it to Mum. She'd have a fit. I plan to do another one showing death and that will really freak her out!

Then, on Thursday evening, when I've given up hope, Finn phones me.

'How are things?'

'Fine.'

'Good.' (Long pause—this is terrible—I've had all these amazing imaginary conversations with him in my head but now it's for real—nothing!)

'Can I pick you up after school tomorrow?' he asks.

'Yes, OK.' I am too surprised and delighted to say more.

We arrange where to meet and I float upstairs like an angel on a pink cloud until I realize that I will be in my school uniform.

Being clothed in cabbage green really worries me right up until I see him. He is standing waiting for me, tall and dark in his old jacket, and I suddenly find that I am running and not walking.

'Hi!' I say breathlessly, then I look at the car he is standing next to and add: 'Where's the van?'

'This is mine. I got rid of the bike.' He walks around and opens the passenger door for me.

'Why did you get rid of the bike? I thought—' I just stop myself from saying 'I thought you loved it'.

He shrugs. 'It was OK for taking your mates out on. But . . . ' He doesn't finish the sentence.

'I would have thought it was really good fun having a bike. The freedom of the road, that sort of thing.'

'Yeah, but . . . not if . . . I mean, if you want to take a girl out a car is better.' He isn't looking at me. He is sitting in the driving seat, holding on to the steering wheel and frowning.

'Oh. I see,' I say. And for a horrible minute I wonder if I have got myself all excited for nothing. Maybe all he is offering me is a lift home. Maybe he wanted to show off his new car to someone and thought I would do. 'Well— it's a very nice car,' I say quietly.

'I thought, maybe, that when you have your birthday in the spring I could teach you to drive it,' he says. 'If you'd like to . . . ' He glances at me quickly. And I feel such a fool because after all the time I've spent thinking about him, and analysing every word in every conversation we've ever had, I haven't worked out that he is shy.

'I'd love that,' I say and I lean over and slip my arms around his neck. 'Thank you,' I whisper. And I'm not sure if I kiss him, or he kisses me, or if we both move at exactly the same moment. But, whatever happened, when we meet up it feels absolutely right and amazing: like diving off the high board, or getting the hang of windsurfing, or imagining you are a seabird gliding on thermals high in the sky.

We are brought down to earth by an irritable tapping on the side window. A furious beetroot face looms. It's The Frog.

I wind down the window.

'Please remember, Jade, that while you are in school uniform you are upholding the reputation and standing of the school. I do not know what the people in these houses must think of all this . . . '

'Right you are, Miss Froggit,' I cut in quickly, and Finn does a fast reverse and we pull away before she can say anything else.

'Sorry,' Finn says, glancing at me. He is trying to look serious but he's grinning all over his face.

'It's OK,' I say with a mock sigh of despair. Nothing is ever going to really get me down again. (Not now.) 'I think she's stalking me—she caught me giving Jack a hug once and now she's convinced I'm a nymphomaniac.'

We giggle all the way back to my house. He parks in the driveway where no one can see us. We arrange to go to the cinema later and he kisses me again (and this time he definitely makes the first move—it's brilliant). I am so pleased I didn't take the advice in the book and practise kissing on my hand. It's much more fun practising on Finn. I am so full of joy that I am singing to myself as I wander into the kitchen.

Then I realize Mum and Dad are sitting at the kitchen table, looking all serious. I just know they are waiting for me. They have decided this is the time to tell me. I can't bear it—not now when I am so happy! My heart sinks.

'I told you Finn was giving me a lift, didn't I?' I say.

'Yes,' Mum says, she looks vacant eyed, as if she's overdosing on worry.

'We're going to the cinema later on, if that's OK?' I see a glance of panic pass between them.

'That's fine,' Dad says. 'There's just something we need to tell you, Jade. It's nothing bad. It's probably something we should have told you a long time ago. It's just we're pretty sure Finn knows about it and . . . ' Dad's chin wobbles and his eyes fill. Mum covers his hand with hers.

'It's me really that needs to tell you, Jadey.'

I've always had an open mind about Guardian Angels. And the strangest thing happens because I get a visit from one. It's a funny kind of angel, but then it's a funny old world. Nana, she of the poison tongue, manifests herself in my mind. Nana, who rewrites history so well. Nana, who thinks she knows everything and knows nothing. I realize now why she has been haunting me. She does have some divine purpose other than being a pain in the butt. She will be my alibi, my life-lie, my genie in the bottle. I know just what to say.

'Now,' my tone is firm, 'we're not going to waste time raking over the past, are we? You're not going to tell me all that old stuff about you not being sure whether I belong to Dad or to your Spanish boyfriend. Because it's all a load of old cobblers.'

They look gutted. I press on, making the most of my advantage. 'It's absolute rubbish. Of course I'm Dad's daughter. We may not look much alike but we're like two peas from a pod. He's fantastic at drawing—you've always said he should have been an architect—and I've inherited that amazing talent of his.' (Modesty goes right out of the window.) 'And how many people know entire sketches from *Fawlty Towers* off by heart?' I move across to Dad and give him a couple of feed lines. He valiantly responds: a watery-eyed Basil to my strident Sybil.

'We like all the same things—the same TV programmes, the same food—even dogs,' I add proudly. 'I think I'm getting more like Dad as I get older. The other day I even squashed all the old soap together to make a new bar and I've started going around the house switching all the lights off. So it's obvious which genetic pool I'm from! I'm really much more like you than Mum, when you think about it,' I say to Dad, and I hug him really hard so he can't look into my eyes.

'Who told you?' Mum manages to mutter.

'Nana,' I say coolly. 'You know what a suspicious mind she's got. She told me years ago—when I was about fourteen. I think she was kind of warning me. She did it for the best. Don't ever say anything to her about it, will you? I swore I'd never tell you.' I open my eyes wide and smile at them. I'm getting really good at acting. It must be Sybil's influence. My voice is kindly as I continue. 'She *is* an old lady, after all, with a dicky ticker. It wouldn't do to upset her. And I promise you it has never bothered me at all. I've never had any doubts. I know I'm Dad's daughter. So let's just forget all about it, shall we? And get on with our lives.'

They look at me, and then they look at each other, and it's as if some great weight has been lifted off their shoulders. 'Supper's nearly ready,' Mum says. They look at each other again and smile. 'I think I might have a glass of sherry as I dish up,' she says.

Dad pours himself a beer, makes me a weak shandy, and gives Mum a sherry. You'd think they'd won the lottery or something fabulous and we were having a drink to celebrate. Dad starts telling me about Murphy and his training class. 'He's going to make a first rate dog. He knows what the instructor is going to say before he's said it. He's not just intelligent—he's a blinking genius.'

They are so happy it makes me want to cry—because I am happy too.

## Postscript

Sybil is only suspended for a week on the condition that she sees a counsellor. Her shrink says she should have a meeting with Jack and me to apologize.

It's terrible because she turns it into a kind of confessional. She says she was jealous of me from the first moment The Frog asked me to look after her because it was obvious that The Frog really liked me. (I feel like interrupting and saying 'not any more' but Sybil's in full flood by this time.) She says that meeting my parents made her jealousy worse. Evidently her mother never once collected her from school and nannies and au pair girls looked after her when she was little.

Jack and I sit in embarrassed silence while Sybil blubs on about what a rotten life she's had and how she doesn't have any friends. Mrs Williams hands her Kleenex and nods kindly. Afterwards Jack says he feels sorry for her, but I don't buy it myself—there again I think I'm a bit of a sympathy-free-zone where Sybil is concerned.

I wonder what would have happened if I had stood up and told them the truth about my family but I wasn't going to do that. The only person who I talk to about it is Finn.

Things are great at home. We manage to keep the house (just!). Dad says it's going to be second-hand cars and no foreign holidays for a couple of years. But that suits me fine because I don't really want to go away for weeks on end and leave Finn.

Dad's new business really takes off—he tells everyone why it's called Jade Homes. And when I hear him say, 'I named it after my daughter', in this really proud voice, I know I have done the right thing in pretending he really is my father. Sometimes I even start to believe it myself . . .

Finn says that everything in life has a good and a bad side. And that applies to lies as well as to bacteria and people. And I know that the lie I told Mum and Dad was a good lie and has made them, and me, happier.

Life is strange. One very spooky thing that happens is that I send Mum's little book to The Frog as an early (and anonymous) Christmas present. And then the unbelievable happens. At the end of term The Frog announces that she is getting married! Even the staff are openly astonished and we all start collecting money to buy her a present. I start thinking that maybe the book works as a kind of lucky charm and helps you find the love of your life. If I'm feeling really generous I might buy one for Sybil just to show there are no hard feelings.

Also by Julia Clarke

## Summertime Blues
ISBN 0 19 275196 4

*It's amazing how much I can glean from listening to one half of a
telephone conversation. I hear whisper, whisper, and then, slowly, half
sentences . . . Then the penny drops. The realization that my parents are
fighting over me, and that neither of them wants me, hits me like a blow
in the belly.*

This is the start of a long, painful summer for Alex. He has no
choice but to go to Yorkshire with his mother and her new partner,
away from his friends, his home, and his A level studies. He just
knows he is going to hate it all, the isolation and quiet of the
countryside, the cold, primitive cottage, and most of all, Seth. His
one thought is to get away, back to civilization in London. But
then he meets Louie, who looks after abandoned and ill-treated
animals, and Faye, Seth's daughter, and suddenly the summer is
full of new experiences and challenges which will change Alex's
life for ever.

'Clarke sharply conveys the sadness and frustration of an only
child who doubts if his existence is worthwhile.'
*The Times*

'A readable and revealing account of growing up.'
*Kids Out*

'written with such pace, humour and believable, adolescent angst
that I found it both moving and compelling.'
*Books for Keeps*

## You Lose Some, You Win Some

ISBN 0 19 275327 4

*Day One of Mum being away and the battle lines of our life have been drawn. No comfort—no crying—no kissing: because nothing is wrong— is it?*

Cesca refuses to accept that Mum has gone. She's just helping out at the hotel, isn't she? Because of the foot-and-mouth outbreak? She'll be back soon and everything will get back to normal, won't it?

But then Cesca learns the secret that has split up her family and she has to believe that Mum has gone for good. How can she cope with everything that is going on—the aftermath of the foot-and-mouth epidemic and the loss of their animals; her on/off relationship with Jon—when Mum is not there to help her? And how will the rest of the family manage: Dad and Gerry and Ollie, who is just a baby? Trying to come to terms with all this, Cesca has to find a strength she didn't know she had . . .

# Chasing Rainbows

ISBN 0 19 275326 6

*It is while I am in Ash's kitchen that the idea comes to me. An arranged marriage could be a very good thing. For a parent, that is . . .*

Rose is full of plans to marry off her scatty, poetic mother to Ralph, their efficient doctor neighbour—after all, opposites attract, don't they? And Ash, Ralph's son, is her best friend—what could be more natural? And when Rose's two young cousins are dumped on them in the holidays, this seems a good opportunity to convince Ralph that her mum would make a perfect doctor's wife.

But Cara and Crystal turn out to be the cousins from hell, and when Hamish comes on the scene it seems that all Rose's schemes will come to nothing. But it is not until her friendship with Ash is threatened that Rose begins to realize that trying to arrange other people's lives is not always a good thing.

Other Oxford novels for young adults:

## Starseeker

Tim Bowler

*Winner of the Carnegie Medal*

ISBN 0 19 275305 3

Luke is in trouble. Skin and the gang have a job for him. They
want him to break into Mrs Little's house and steal the jewellery
box. They want him to prove that he's got what it takes. That he's
part of the gang.

But Luke finds more than just a jewellery box in the house. He
finds something so unexpected it will change his life forever . . .

*This is a wonderful, rich novel, written with lyricism, drama, and power.*
*Tackling issues of loss, love, and healing, and filled with the sense of a*
*universe bursting with music, it is unputdownable from the first page to*
*the last.*

'A thundering read, full of challenging ideas, strong emotions,
and layers of plotting.'
Lindsey Fraser, *The Guardian*

'A fantastic book.'
> *Sunday Express*

'Compelling and suspenseful.'
> *Sunday Times*

### Forbidden

Judy Waite

ISBN 0 19 275312 6

*Something scratches at my memory that I cannot break the surface of, but I know that its roots run back to the time when Howard first made me one of his Chosen. A Bad Thing happened then.*

Elinor is lucky. So lucky. She's been chosen.

She's waited for this moment all her life. She will give herself to the man she loves. Willingly sacrifice her innocence for him.

People on the outside don't understand. They can't feel love like the Followers do. And the end is coming. It's so close now.

But a chance meeting in the woods could alter the course of Elinor's destiny. She must resist . . . she must.

## Never Ever

Helena Pielichaty

ISBN 0 19 275261 8

*Erin can't stand living on the estate. She wishes she could go back to her old house, with its nice garden, her own room, and a phone! She can't stand living near Liam Droy either—he's such a jerk. He may be good-looking, but he knows it—and everyone knows that looks aren't everything.*

Liam loves life on the estate. Well, he is the king round here, after all. The girls adore him, the boys respect him. And now Erin Mackiness has moved in down the road, things couldn't be better. She's playing it cool, but surely it's only a matter of time before she gives in to his charms . . .

'*Never Ever* is a wonderfully honest tale of teenage life. At times painfully sad and downright hilarious, Helena Pielichaty has captured the teen voices of these characters perfectly.'

*Ottakar's Young Adult Book of the Month*

'Pielichaty has written a witty and entertaining story'

*Books for Keeps*